# WESTWARD

# Also by Ron Briggs

**Yellow Hair Series**

*Erik Haraldsson*

*Tor's Saga*

*Cass*

# WESTWARD

## YELLOW HAIR
### BOOK FOUR

## RON BRIGGS

**WOLFPACK**
**PUBLISHING**
— EST 2013 —

**Westward**
Paperback Edition
Copyright © 2024 by Ron Briggs

Wolfpack Publishing
1707 E. Diana Street
Tampa, Florida 33609

www.wolfpackpublishing.com

Paperback ISBN 979-8-89567-087-3
Ebook ISBN 979-8-89567-086-6
LCCN 2024949144

# FOREWORD

This is a work of fiction. The characters, events, and places are contrived by the author. An honest attempt has been made to describe real cultures and interactions as they may have taken place early in the eleventh century CE.

The cultures depicted as interacting in this story are the Norwegian Norse, Greenlandic Norse, Icelandic Norse, riverine Lenape, Monongahela, Late Fort Ancient, Ilini, and Owasco or proto-Iroquois (also called Haudenosaunee by some).

The descriptions reflect the transition from Middle Woodland to Late Woodland traditions and touches on the blossoming of the Mississippian culture that would have a great influence over the next several generations.

This fourth book of the series features the

young Norseman, Yellow Hair, meeting the Monongahela maiden who has recently destroyed the evil war chief who had killed her parents. The two find themselves destined to journey to the growing community known as Cahokia by modern archaeologists, although no one knows for sure what they called their great city.

Some notes on Cahokia and this author's version presented in this book: It is accepted that Cahokia experienced a population, cultural, and construction explosion around 1050 to 1100 CE. A catalyst for the changes may well have been a supernova visible in the daytime sky across North America that lasted several days in 1054 CE.

A lesser known, but possibly just as important supernova occurred in 1004 CE. Documentation from around the world supports the event. Some archaeologists believe the earlier supernova trig-gered the concentration of power in the American Bottom where Cahokia existed as a large village of farmers and traders with probably less than a thousand year-round inhabitants at the time. Some fifty years later, the city had blossomed to many times that size, possibly as many as twenty thousand in the central heart of the metropolis and many more in outlying districts.

This story suggests an interim period when population and culture were being consolidated and powerful families and clans were putting plans in place to control future growth and political power. This version of the history of Cahokia is a product of the author's imagination. Any connection to actual events and artifacts is purely coincidental. It is the author's intention and hope that the setting is accurately described.

# WESTWARD

WESTWARD

# CHAPTER 1
# MEETING

Yellow Hair watched the young woman seemingly float over the canoes lying along the top of the riverbank. She hurdled those overturned dugouts like a deer running through a forest of deadfalls. They were passing by where she came to the river's edge waving her arms frantically and calling Traveler's name. Yellow Hair's focus was on her muscular legs, arms, and short-cropped hair, paying no attention to the river as they coasted by her. He was so entranced that Traveler had to yell his name to get his attention.

"Yellow Hair! She wanted us to beach where there is an open slot!" Traveler scolded Yellow Hair as he shrugged his shoulders toward Cass.

Jerking back to the situation, Yellow Hair drove

his paddle into the swift river and started a sharp turn that would bring them around to where the young woman was standing on the riverbank. He needed all his strength to make the loop while fighting the current. Just when they were moving toward the slot she indicated, a pinprick of an opening in the overcast sky put bright sunlight into his face, momentarily blinding him. But he managed to fight through the distraction and propel the canoe to the river bank right next to the young woman.

The canoe slid to a stop, and Yellow Hair, in one motion, stowed his paddle, clutched the gunwales, and threw his hips over the side, landing on both feet next to the craft. He then stepped forward, grasped the front thwart, and pulled the entire canoe out of the river with Traveler still sitting in the rear. Yellow Hair steadied the canoe while Traveler stepped out.

Yellow Hair turned to go back and help his partner. He stopped short, less than two paces from the young woman. She was standing, looking at him with a wide smile across her face. It gave him a chance to see her features closely for the first time. Her muscular body was covered with smooth skin that reminded him of sanded, polished, and oiled butternut heartwood. Her face was egg-shaped, with a smooth, bold forehead bordered on top by black hair less than a fingernail long and thin, arching black eyebrows. Her high cheekbones tapered smoothly down to a smallish but strong chin. Her full lips were bent into a broad smile, baring straight, white teeth. Her smile creased deep dimples into her slender cheeks. Her nose was small, straight, and slightly upturned. Then there were the eyes. Those eyes. Bottomless pools of liquid obsidian. He paid no attention to her faded brown shirt stained by animal fat and blood.

*Surely God has never breathed life into a more perfect creature!* He felt a strange warmth flow through his entire body as he peered into her eyes.

————

CASS HURDLED seven canoes before reaching the open slot. She stood at the water's edge, frantically waving her arms and jumping up and down while yelling to Traveler. He shouted something to the man in front, and they started a loop that would bring them back to her—if they did not swamp in the river rushing up to its banks.

"Greetings, trader! My heart soars to see you! I thought you had been eaten by a whale in the Eastern Ocean!" Cass cheerfully called to Traveler while the canoe turned to approach her position.

When the craft straightened to come ashore

where she stood, a pinprick of a hole opened in the clouds that had hid the sun all day. A single beam of bright sunlight shone on the front of Traveler's canoe.

Cass was stunned. "What is it?" she mumbled. *It looks like a man. A very powerful man!* She watched the muscles ripple through his broad shoulders and arms as he pulled his paddle through the brown water, accelerating the craft toward the bank. *But no man has such pale skin! And hair the color of aspen leaves in the early autumn? Legends talk of such, but no one has ever seen one.*

The bark canoe slid over the lip of the riverbank and to a stop. The "thing" smoothly stowed his paddle, clutched the sides of the boat with big hands, and threw muscular legs out to the side. He landed, muscles rippling in those powerful legs, stepped forward, grasped the front cross-brace, and with a powerful effort, pulled the whole craft out of the river while Traveler still sat in his place in the rear.

*I think it is a man.*

His broad shoulders accented his narrow waist and strong legs. He straightened, turned, and started for her. She could only smile, mesmerized. Now, she could study his features. His head was almost rectangular. She noted that he wore no tattoos. A smooth, bold forehead was bordered on the top by that yellow hair. It had been plaited into a single large braid that hung down his back, and his full eyebrows were a few shades lighter than his hair. His high cheekbones barely tapered to a powerful jaw. His full lips were bent into a wide smile., baring large, straight, white teeth. His wide smile creased his cheeks into deep dimples. Another dimple was centered in his full chin. His nose was proportionately large and almost straight with only a small hump and slight crook, as if his nose had been broken sometime in the past. Then there were his eyes. Those eyes. Bottomless pools of liquid blue sky.

*Surely the Creator has never breathed life into a more perfect creature! Never has a man looked right into my souls! And I can see his souls are pure and good.* She felt a warmth run through her body she had never known. She was reminded of her own words to Corn Stalk: "The eagle looks into his mate's eyes as an equal."

———

AFTER SPENDING some time directing Red Oak's men about transporting the canoe's contents to the village, Traveler walked up and assessed the situation. He noticed that Yellow Hair could not take his eyes off Cass. And her eyes were glued on Yellow Hair. *This will be interesting.*

"Greetings, warrior. Allow me to introduce my companion here. His name is Yellow Hair. He is of the Norse Clan from a land called Norway. He has come a long way to meet you." He talked fast enough so that Yellow Hair would not understand many of his words and seemed to pay no attention.

She was still staring into Yellow Hair's eyes. At Traveler's suggestion, she held her right hand out toward Yellow Hair, palm up. "I-I-I am Cass."

Yellow Hair looked at her extended hand, and suddenly, a flashback hit him. When the beautiful *shieldmaiden* who would be Master of one of the dragon ships they had built at the Ulfrstadt ship-works was brought forward, his father greeted the woman by taking her hand and kissing the middle knuckle.

Yellow Hair took the hand that was extended toward him, turned it over, lifted it slightly, bowed his head, and gently kissed her middle knuckle. When he straightened back up, he saw that her expression never changed. She still gazed at him with that wide smile on her face. The young woman limply dropped her arm when he reluctantly let go of her hand.

Traveler looked at Cass, shocked that she let the foreigner kiss her hand, waiting for her to say more. Her gaze never faltered but stayed glued to Yellow Hair's eyes. He stepped closer and grabbed both young people by the arm and turned them toward the trail to the Monongahela Village palisade opening. By now, the small hole in the clouds had expanded greatly. As if by some witchery, the clouds began to evaporate.

"Let us finish with the introductions in Corn Stalk's longhouse." Traveler turned to Cass, shaking his head. "So how is your training coming along, Cass?"

"You have been traveling with Red Hand, so you know that I have finished what Wolf tasked me to do. My 'training,' as you call it, is over." Her reply was without humor, and she kept her trance-like smile and her eyes on the big yellow-haired man to her left.

"Yes, well, I want to hear the whole story from you. I especially want to know what happened to your hair. Then, I will tell you Yellow Hair's story. He is not fully familiar with your tongue yet. I have been teaching him, but he still has a lot to learn. Perhaps over the next few days you can help me— payment for your war club and all." His sly smile was unnoticed by anyone but himself.

"So, is Red Hand here to make peace with Monongahela Village?" Cass asked Traveler, her concentration on Yellow Hair never wavering.

"He is, and with the Long Pines. His main purpose here is to ask Pena if she will accept him as her husband. He wants to be part of the new Long Pine Village."

"She goes by her old name now, *Bright Star*. Red Hand told me what happened to his wife and child." Traveler caught a touch of sadness in her voice.

"Always a tragedy when a child is lost, and a young woman dies like that." Traveler's voice echoed sorrow.

# CHAPTER 2
# CASS AND YELLOW HAIR

They arrived at the longhouse at the same time Bright Star came running in from the fields dirty and sweaty. She quickly greeted Traveler, totally ignoring Cass and Yellow Hair, as she ducked through the door hanging into the longhouse. Cass, Traveler, and Yellow Hair followed.

Introductions of the Monongahela Village people present took nearly two fingers of time, and when they were done, Night Owl, Head Matron of Black Bear Village went through a lengthy introduction of the Black Bear Village people present, followed by a dissertation on the history of Black Bear Village and how their late war chief came to power and on and on. She finished with the Black Bear account of how the war chief's days of power ended. She commended Cass and Bright Star for selecting only warriors loyal to the late war chief and not those who wanted peace. She then asked Cass to tell her story. When Cass was finished, the sun was setting.

Night Owl asked Corn Stalk to meet with her in private. Corn Stalk granted the private meeting and told everyone else to be back in one hand of time for a feast.

Traveler, War Chief Wolf Master, Red Oak, Red Hand, Ten Point, Tallow, and some other warriors settled into a long discussion about the happenings in the east and north. Bright Star and Water Mint took Red Hand outside to talk. Cass turned to Yellow Hair and asked him to step outside using signs and simple words.

They stepped out to a brilliant, almost-full moon coming up over the eastern hills and shining through the treetops. The evening sky was now cloudless, and stars were a sparkling blanket from horizon to horizon. As the moon rose just above the hills, it appeared huge. Cass pointed to the yellow orb. "Planter's Moon. The moon our women plant the three sisters."

Yellow Hair replied with some difficulty, "Yes, plant corn. Bright Moon—more you face."

She looked away. *My old name never sounded so good, even though he was referring to the real moon.*

10

*What is happening to me?* When she looked back at him, she could not help but smile.

"Yellow Hair say wrong?" he asked clumsily, sounding embarrassed.

"No, Yellow Hair say good—very good." She smiled coyly.

As they strolled across the plaza, she took his hand in hers. His smile widened. A small stand of White Cedar trees appeared as they approached the edge of the plaza opposite the Corn Clan longhouse. Suddenly, a big figure stepped in front of them.

"I will lead you away from this vile foreigner, Maiden Cass." Many Feathers stood tall, pride in his voice.

"You will not lead me anywhere. Yellow Hair and I are enjoying the moonlight. Now, if you would leave us, please."

"Sorry, I cannot do that, maiden. Many Feathers is duty bound to protect his future wife from worm-rotted intruders." The warrior put his hand on his war club and took an aggressive stance.

"Yellow Hair hears some of your words, Many Feathers. He thinks you should walk a new trail. Trouble will only come here if you stay." Yellow Hair struggled putting words together.

"You talk like the fool you are, foreigner. I

suggest you walk a new trail. Forget this maiden—she will be mine."

"Come, Yellow Hair. Many Feathers knows not what he is saying." Looking at Many Feathers, she pointed to the Corn Clan longhouse.

"Not so fast, maiden." Many Feathers stepped closer to Cass and reached for her arm.

The instant his hand clasped her arm, a swift leg swept his feet from under him, and he landed on his butt on the packed dirt. Yellow Hair started toward Many Feathers, but Cass put her hand up to stop him.

"No need for this to go any further." Cass looked down at the shocked warrior with fierce eyes. "Understand that I am not your property and never will be. Now, go back to the longhouse before you get embarrassed."

In the corner of her eye, Cass caught a movement. Suddenly, Yellow Hair whirled and drove a big fist into the side of the short warrior Cold Duck's head. The warrior crumbled like the turkey she had once killed with a thrown stone to the head. Cold Duck lay on the ground, unmoving.

"Did you kill him?" Many Feathers demanded while getting himself up off the ground.

Cass felt Cold Duck's neck. "No, he is just resting." She smiled inwardly at Yellow Hair's awareness, speed, and power.

Shortly, Cold Duck regained consciousness, though quite disoriented. Many Feathers helped him to his feet. "Come, friend, let us leave these crazy people."

Many Feathers turned to Cass and snarled, "Take your brutish foreigner! I hope he beats you to death. That is surely what you deserve, mankiller." His tone was one of total disdain.

Cass guided Yellow Hair back across the plaza. "We should get back to Corn Stalk's longhouse." She waved across the plaza, never letting go of his muscular arm.

When they walked back into the longhouse, Cass took her place beside Bright Star to the right of Water Mint and her family on the right side of the firepit. Yellow Hair sat to Traveler's left on the left side of the firepit. Night Owl, Red Loon, Goldeneye, Red Hand, Ten Point, and Two Hearts sat in the honored guests' positions to Corn Stalk's left side. Family members were to the right.

Corn Stalk directed her servants to feed the guests fresh venison stew, sweetened corn cakes, and sassafras tea sweetened with fresh blackberries. As promised, Cass passed her two corn cakes to Sprout, who nodded a thank you.

After the feast, Traveler related Yellow Hair's story from his homeland to the present. The faces reflected disbelief. All but one, hers reflected awe.

The war chief wanted to know why, if he had killed enemies, Yellow Hair still wore his hair full. "Lenape warriors who had killed other men wear only a scalp lock somewhere on their head."

Through Traveler's interpretation, Yellow Hair explained that it was not part of his family's traditions, and he did not want to shave his head. Men in his family were proud of a full head of long hair. Yellow Hair explained further that some members of his nation do shave parts of their heads, sometimes as a ritual. The war chief looked away, feeling embarrassed for Yellow Hair.

"And tattoos? Do warriors in your lands earn tattoos?" the war chief inquired.

"Some do. Again, my father never did. I cannot say why, but I have not, so far, to honor him." After a short pause, "I did not take any body decorations among the Lenape because I did not feel I belonged there. In the future? I cannot say."

———

THE NEXT MORNING Cass found Traveler at the canoe landing alone, painting boiled pinesap on the seams of his bark canoe. He wore an old buckskin shirt, tattered leggings, and an old breechclout. She wore the same sleeveless, brown fabric hunting shirt, tied at the waist with a hemp sash, and a doeskin loincloth. The day promised to be warm and sunny.

"Greetings, trader. Are you enjoying your stay in Monongahela Village? It appears that you have warmed the Head Matron's blankets again. She must admire you."

"As I admire her, but that is between her and me." He considered the subject closed.

"Between you? You do know that everyone from Willet Village to Cahokia speaks of it, do you not?"

"I see no reason to deny nor confirm any rumors about where I sleep. Now, on a serious matter. What are your plans, Cass? Will you help build New Long Pine Village? You are a hero, highly respected, and somewhat of a seer, I hear. You could be the first woman shaman in the new village."

"I do not know. I can see Bright Star's future, and it is full of clan responsibilities and children. She will always be the responsible one. My future is a gray cloud. I just feel...well, lost...like my reason for being here...for living...is gone. I do not feel like I belong here—or anywhere—anymore." After a pause. "What is it like in the west?" Once again something came out of her mouth as if another person had said it. She did not want to tip her hand about how she felt about Yellow Hair.

"I think I can be totally honest with you, Cass. Promise me this conversation will go nowhere beyond your ears."

"I promise." A flicker of life shone in the darkness that clouded her mind.

"I saw the sparks flying between you and Yellow Hair. I think you and he would get along famously. But I want you to know that his future is uncertain. I am bound to take him to a very powerful man. I do not think that man would be happy at all if I brought Yellow Hair before him with a mate. It could endanger both of you. If I can demonstrate that Yellow Hair is an ordinary man, not some sort of a god or messenger from the sky gods, I think I can get him away from that powerful man. I promised Yellow Hair that if I can do that, I will try to get him back to people from his homeland. I do not know how, but I know some people to ask."

He refocused his gaze into her curious eyes. "Back to you. If you could go along and not get in the way of my maneuvering, I will be happy to bring you to Cahokia. Until I have Yellow Hair freed from The Great Sun, you must stay out of his blankets. You could play the part of my slave when we arrive in Cahokia," he said, looking unblinking into her eyes. The same determination that existed before her meeting with Thunder Throat was back.

16

He knew she was coming along. "If all happens the way I hope, you and Yellow Hair will be with each other as long as you wish."

"I can do whatever is needed of me, Traveler. I think you know that much about me." Her tone was suddenly confident. "But surely you know that Yellow Hair and me, well, there is something between us. There will be no way that I can stay away from his blankets all the way to Cahokia. That is asking too much."

"If Yellow Hair shows up in Cahokia with a pregnant wife, Far Gazer will have him sacrificed without hesitation. He has been waiting more than four sun cycles for Yellow Hair's arrival. He would take that as an insult, I am sure." Traveler looked into her eyes, trying to convey the gravity of his words.

"Surely you know that I have enough knowledge of plants to keep from letting a seed being planted in my womb. I was not born yesterday."

"No, I did not know you were so experienced. Corn Stalk claims she is worried that you have no interest in the young warriors. She hears rumors of you being two spirit and worries about your future as a matron in your clan."

"Ha, she sends predators to me and expects me to fall in love! And, no, I do not have *experience*, myself, but I pay attention and watched my sister as she fell in love with Red Hand. They were coupling like foxes every time they got together for three sun cycles. I know how to use squawroot. You need not worry about that.

"You can also talk to Water Mint if you like. She may be my Head Matron now, not that I need her permission." A pause. "Where is Yellow Hair this morning?"

"He and Tallow took Fingerling and Dewdrop fishing. You will find Yellow Hair is quite popular with the little ones. They like his yellow hair, I think." He smiled slyly, knowing she liked it too.

"Yes, but have you looked into those deep blue eyes?" She laughed, not knowing where the words came from.

Traveler just smiled and shook his head. *What kind of trouble have I gotten myself into this time? Two people I care about are in love, but am I leading them to their deaths?*

———

MIDWAY THROUGH THE AFTERNOON, Tallow and Yellow Hair came racing through the palisade wall and toward Corn Stalk's longhouse. Cass, wearing only a breechclout and a clean, thin fabric shirt, was sitting on a stump with an elk skin pad over one muscular thigh pressing a deer antler tine against the edge of the obsidian knife she had taken from Thunder Throat. She was all but finished putting a new, razor-sharp edge on the knife by flaking off tiny fragments along the cutting edge.

Tallow and Fingerling were racing one another while Yellow Hair was bounding along with little Dewdrop on his back, getting her to laugh hysterically with every little jump. Tallow carried a reed bag that was wet and slightly bulged in the middle.

"Did the men catch the fish, or did you?" Cass smiled into Fingerling's eyes.

"I caught...one, but Dewdrop did not get any!" His big brown eyes beaming as he answered excitedly and shyly at the same time.

"You are helping feed us! Just like a grown warrior." Her compliment brought a wider smile to the boy's face.

Her eyes met Yellow Hair's. For the first time since Rock Ridge, she saw a future. And she could tell he saw it too.

*I do not know if I can stay out of that man's blankets until things are settled in Cahokia. I hope it does not take long. Who am I kidding, we will probably be tangled in a blanket somewhere in the forest tonight!*

She noted his eyes flicker toward her chest, and for the first time in her life, she felt like a woman who wanted to be desired. She wiped the blade on the elk skin pad, slid the knife back into its sheath, put her antler tool in its leather bag resting against the log she was sitting on, stood up as she shook the fine flakes of obsidian from the elk skin pad onto the ground next to the base of the longhouse wall, folded it, and placed it in the bag. Then she looked at the men. "Want some tea?" Next, she turned so Yellow Hair had a clear view of her firm breast and protruding nipple.

Tallow was embarrassed by her forwardness. *She does not have to flaunt herself. He swallowed her hook before she even let the line out. I will talk to Water Mint about that. But Yellow Hair and Traveler are leaving for Cahokia in two days. Could be trouble...*

As they crossed the reed mats on the longhouse floor, Tallow heard Cass say to Yellow Hair, "We talk." A tinge of jealousy slipped into Tallow's mind.

———

AFTER AN EVENING OF STORYTELLING, the guests left the longhouse. Everyone staying there rolled out their sleeping blankets. Cass and Yellow Hair slipped out into the moonlight. The moon was now full and just as bright as the night before. She looked up at the bright sphere. "My name was once *Bright Moon*, a long time past."

He looked into her shining black eyes and took her hand. "I know. Why not change? Bright Moon fit you. Names mean person...Yellow Hair not know words...name mean who person is. Bright Moon is you." He pointed to the moon and to her. She smiled and decided to change back to her childhood name—for a man—just as Bright Star had. That would have to come after things were settled in Cahokia.

"Yellow Hair angry if Cass go with him to Cahokia? Traveler will tell Yellow Hair all about it."

He nodded his head vehemently. "Yellow Hair share canoe with Bright Moon! Yes!" His whole body smiled.

"Good!" She led him through the palisade and out to a small clearing she knew about. Once there, she spread the blanket she had discreetly taken from the longhouse. The couple embraced, and after a long, passionate kiss, Cass confessed, "I have never known a man. I-I...am not sure w-what to do." She looked down at the blanket, not wanting him to see the tears in her eyes. She wanted to make him happy but did not know how.

From his memory, he recalled what Stinger had told him, "It is easy to learn." His swollen, throbbing manhood was painfully confined in his tough buckskin breechclout. "B-but if y-you w-want to w-wait, I will understand."

"We are here now." She stepped back and slipped her shirt over her head before dropping her loincloth. Then, she stepped up and began pulling off his lightweight fabric shirt and breechclout. The size of his manhood caught her by surprise. She had seen Tallow naked a few times, even as he and Water Mint were preparing to make love. But never close up, like she was seeing Yellow Hair.

He kissed her again, long and tenderly, before easing her to the blanket. After that kiss, she was ready for anything. But Yellow Hair gently laid her back and kissed her again. He began to explore her body with his hands. Her body put Stinger's to shame.

Each new place he slid his hand caused Cass to suck in a breath. She whimpered when his big hand cupped her breast with its hard, throbbing nipple. She slid her hand down and slipped it along his hardened shaft. The warmth of the tender skin made her want him all the more. When she discovered his wetness, she was taken aback slightly. Then she remembered Pena talking about how messy the process of lovemaking for the first time seemed. Cass just slid that moisture down and rubbed it across his manhood and pulled him on top of her.

"Are you ready?" Yellow Hair asked breathlessly. He found her moist opening but to his surprise, she was already guiding him into her. He eased into her as gently as he could, but she demanded he be more forceful. She soon had her hands on his buttocks and was desperately pulling him into her.

After a few clumsy thrusts, they found their rhythm and ecstasy overwhelmed them both. Cass, her eyes pinched closed, witnessed colorful rainbows exploding in her vision as her woman muscles clamped onto his hardness, sending waves of adrenaline-aided pleasure radiating out from her loins and through her entire body.

Yellow Hair endured holding his breath as she pulled him deeper and deeper into her. Finally, he could hold back no longer, and he pumped his entire soul into her. Even as he did, her legs wrapped around his thighs like she would never let go.

Both completely spent, they rolled to their sides, held each other, and panted until some semblance of breath returned to their heaving lungs.

"There is no doubt that gods have brought us together." Cass panted, slowly relaxing. Her voice was hoarse, barely above a whisper.

"Yess!"

"ARE YOU SURE ABOUT THIS, SISTER?" Bright Star asked Cass when she finally got her alone. "The man is a foreign stranger. He cannot even talk in our tongue. You cannot know what he is really like. I am afraid you will be off somewhere far away, and he will abandon you. I could not stand for that to happen to you." The concern in Bright Star's voice was genuine.

"I am as sure of this as I was of the Wolf vision, sister. To begin with, he is no longer a stranger. You should have learned by now that when things come to me, they always happen. Trust me, all will be good. His fate is tied to mine, as mine is to his, and together, good things will happen. Apart— nothing but darkness. I saw that light when I looked into his blue eyes. They say good things. Tonight was one of the best things I could ever have dreamed! For the first time since Rock Ridge, I feel like living. I will change my name back to Bright Moon when all is settled in Cahokia. Does that please you?" Cass looked past Bright Star as she talked. Bright Star could not see the twinkle in her sister's eyes, but she knew it was there.

Bright Star took her sister's hands into hers, looked into her eyes, and said, "Yes!" through tear-filled eyes. The young women embraced and said simultaneously, "I will miss you, sister!"

Bright Star added, "And you will miss my wedding. Maybe you all could stay for the Green Corn Celebration?" Tears dripped on bare shoulders.

Cass sniffed. "Traveler is anxious to arrive in Cahokia and get this thing with Yellow Hair over. He has been gone four sun cycles now. The longer he delays, the harder things will be there, I think."

# CHAPTER 3
# DOWN RIVER

With everything settled the best they could, Traveler, Yellow Hair, and Cass pushed the big birch-bark canoe into the water and started down the Spirit River. The water had dropped several feet in the past four days. If they avoided trouble, they would be in Cahokia in plenty of time before the harvest celebration. Traveler felt like a respected elder sitting in the middle of the canoe while Cass paddled from the front and Yellow Hair from Traveler's usual position in the rear.

On their second day, as Cass stroked, Traveler admired her powerful back and shoulder muscles, bulging, rippling, and flexing—gained from years of paddling up and down the river and other training preparing herself for the fight with

Thunder Throat. By midmorning, the day had warmed considerably. Traveler was surprised when Cass slid her paddle into the space in front of her, wriggled her sash off, and slipped her sweat-soaked hunting shirt over her head. She never turned around, but his imagination envisioned her firm breasts proudly basking in the warm sun's rays.

*Any warrior would be taking their chances in a fight with that one. I cannot remember a woman as strong and agile as her. Remarkable—Yellow Hair is lucky indeed. Or did something other than fate bring these two together?* He pondered that as they rode the current north and westward.

Clouds rolled in with the sunset. With the cooling temperature, Cass casually turned, pulled a long-sleeved buckskin shirt from her personal bag, and pulled it over her head. She made no attempt to hide her naked upper torso from Traveler, whom she considered a kindly uncle.

This night they would travel past the new village Traveler had seen on his trip east. Corn Stalk had said that the village had suffered terrible losses in their raid on Squirrel Tail Village. Long Pipe's defenses were perfectly arranged, and the upstart warriors lost their war chief and his second. They retreated in disarray, losing half of their young warriors. After that, their shaman supposedly had a vision, and the entire village moved to Cahokia.

According to the traders, the village was abandoned. Traveler was not going to take any chances. They would slip past in the middle of the night along the opposite riverbank. The rain moving in would help conceal them. When they passed the village, a lightning bolt revealed tall weeds growing in the entrance of the palisade. No smoke was visible over the pole wall. *I have been gone a long time. More than four sun cycles, by my calculations. Far Gazer is expecting a boy. How will he react to a powerful young man?*

Two days later Traveler saw gray smoke rising above the trees downriver in a familiar location. "We eat a warm meal that we do not have to cook tonight, my friends!"

"What is this place?" Cass asked over her shoulder, using her head to indicate the smoke.

"Squirrel Tail Village. My old friend, Long Pipe, is chief here. You heard Corn Stalk talk of how he defeated the warriors from that abandoned village upriver." Traveler enthusiastically watched for movement from the village.

"Ah, Long Pipe. I have heard his name at Monongahela Village. Some say he warms Matron Corn Stalk's blankets when he visits." She enjoyed teasing Traveler about his sex life.

"He is a good man, and she is a good woman. Why shouldn't they warm each other's blankets? Besides, I cannot be there all the time." He liked the ribald banter with the young woman, as well.

"No, I suppose not. Yellow Hair told me you kept yourself busy in Willet Village and Sun Town as well."

"Why are my blankets so important to you?"

"Trust me, they are not. I just find it amusing that powerful women find you so attractive when you have nothing to offer them, and you are never in one place for long." She tried to comment neutrally but nearly laughed aloud.

"Maybe that is what they like. I am not a man who will make demands in their already busy lives." He was finished with the subject.

A canoe with four young warriors pulled alongside them from behind. Moments later, another came up on the other side. The leader motioned them toward the landing.

"Greetings, warrior!" Traveler called in an accent Cass could barely understand. "Tell my friend, Long Pipe, that Traveler returns."

The warrior smiled recognition at Traveler and his canoe accelerated toward the landing. The other canoe stayed with them. Traveler held his open palm toward the leader in that canoe with a smile. The canoe leader smiled back.

## CHAPTER 4
# SQUIRREL TAIL VILLAGE

"I have no black drink, but this sassafras and berry tea is quite palatable," Long Pipe said after they were all seated in his longhouse and introductions were completed. "You have some interesting companions, Traveler. I think we will be up all night, telling stories—maybe two nights."

"This young man has business in Cahokia. I offered him a seat in my canoe so he would not have to build one. He is paying his passage by paddling. This girl is my slave. I acquired her from a matron who could not afford the copper-inlaid gorget she had to have. I may sell her when we get to Cahokia. I have little use for a slave." Traveler tried to sound convincing. Cass looked at her lap, trying not to let her smile show. Yellow Hair understood few of the words and just smiled and nodded when Long Pipe looked at him.

"Oh, come now, Traveler. Remember, I know you. You can lie better than that!" Long Pipe laughed. "I know all about Cass here and her ordeal with that war chief up on the Spirit Water River. And everyone knows about Yellow Hair; how he washed up on the beach near a place called Willet Village, and how he escaped from Ganeco. Like I said, you have some interesting companions!" Long Pipe's grin went from ear to ear, and his wink seemed to be directed at each person around the fire.

"Your information travels faster than mine, old friend."

"Unusual stories always travel fast downriver. You know all you traders love to be the first to tell a juicy story." Long Pipe snickered as he studied Traveler's companions.

"But, elder, you have not been in Monongahela Village since my *ordeal* with the former war chief of Black Bear Village." Cass jumped into the conversation, arms out, palms up. She did not like the idea of her reputation as a mankiller spreading.

"No. But every trader knows the story by now. It has been more than a moon since your successful war walk, I believe. You cannot keep this kind of story a secret for long." He chuckled as he indicated Traveler. "The river traders are also eager to talk about Yellow Hair. His story is quite unique."

"You are a sly old fox. Tell us about your battle with that new village upriver."

"I suppose you got that from Corn Stalk." Long Pipe looked conspiratorially at his friend.

"Other traders. Tell us about the war. What was his name? Hawk Talon, is that right?"

"That war chief was a young hot head. He got a bunch of other hot heads together and thought they could make the most of the religious changes taking place along the river. He thought his brand of hard raiding would intimidate the old matrons to hold him as a great war chief. He imagined everyone paying him tribute and replacing the old religion with his brand of Horned Serpent worship." Long Pipe took a drag off his pipe to relax and gather his thoughts.

"The problem was that he was an impulsive war chief and took too many chances. We tricked him into dividing his forces, and we were able to cut them to shreds. Their survivors limped back upriver to Hawk Talon Town, as they called it. A short time later, the whole village vacated and moved to Cahokia where they could blend in with the other newcomers there. They went by here with their loaded canoes, but naturally did not stop to tell us their plans. There has been no activity in Hawk Talon Town for nearly three sun cycles. They did not even harvest their corn, and their fields have been untouched ever since.

"I have received no word about how the Illini peoples treated them. The Illini, as you know, are not noted for their hospitality. May I be so bold as to ask if you have a plan to slip this contraband through their watchful eyes? Anyone can see that once her hair grows back, Cass is a raving beauty. And Yellow Hair here, how many unscrupulous chiefs would not want to have a yellow-haired slave around, or on his scalp stick? These two could fetch a pretty sum in some dark corners along the river. And the Illini know where each of those dark places is." He directed his eyes to Traveler while he waved a hand toward Cass and Yellow Hair. Everyone looked questioningly toward Traveler.

He shrugged and quietly said, "I am working on it."

"You can always ask Thunderbird for a heavy rain or maybe a dense fog, I suppose."

"Some power has managed to get Yellow Hair this far," Traveler grinned sheepishly.

"Can you stay long enough to get a chunkey game in?" Long Pipe changed the subject, seeing his friend struggling for a good answer to his last question.

"If we get some sleep," Traveler answered.

Cass and Yellow Hair asked simultaneously "Chunkey?"

"I definitely want to play them... and bet on me!" Long Pipe snickered.

"I believe I will take that bet, Chief," Traveler smiled.

The next day's sun had climbed nearly over the trees when Traveler opened sleepy eyes. He looked over and saw Yellow Hair's and Cass's sleeping skins rolled up and leaning against the longhouse wall. He went outside to relieve himself and heard the familiar sound of a chunkey stone rolling across a packed dirt court. A *thunk* told him a lance had been thrown to its thrower's predicted stopping point of the stone. When the sound of the rolling stone stopped, he heard an exuberant yell in a feminine voice. He knew, as expected, that Cass was learning the game quickly. Finishing his business, he hurried to the source of the sounds.

"How are my students coming along?" Traveler directed the question to Long Pipe but knew the answer.

"Tricked me again, my coyote friend," Long Pipe joked, shaking his head.

Traveler watched Yellow Hair trot to a marked

line on the flat, packed-dirt court, roll the disc-shaped stone smoothly with his left hand, then shift his weight while he ran and threw a lance-shaped stick with a fire hardened end in the direction the stone disc rolled. The lance glided smoothly through the air and landed twenty paces in front and a couple of paces to the right of the rolling disc. The disc slowed, came to a stop, and fell on its side two and a half paces from the lance.

"Ah, too bad, Yellow Hair, I win again!" Cass chided as she went and retrieved her lance and disc, which were less than two paces apart, and almost as far down the court.

"I might have guessed you would bring in a couple of ringers, you thief," Long Pipe complained. "I think we should wager the old men against the young upstarts," he boldly called.

"Do I get any practice rolls?" Traveler asked.

"Do you need any?" Long Pipe asked, smiling mischievously.

"I think we've been had," Yellow Hair said under his breath to Cass. "What is the wager?" he asked Long Pipe.

"Losers have to prepare and maintain the sweat lodge for the winners but cannot use it." Long Pipe grinned and winked at Traveler.

"Who goes first?" Yellow Hair asked eagerly. *It would be nice spending a hand of time or more in the sweat lodge with Bright Moon*. He had taken to thinking of her by her old name, which he considered much prettier than the one she was using.

"We will throw our chunkey sticks as far down the field as we can. We will go in the order of the sticks, longest throw to shortest. Broadleaf, you will judge. Each player gets one chance. Longest combined distance of the teams wins." One of Long Pipe's warriors had come to watch and was drafted as judge.

Yellow Hair ran to the line and cast his lance in a flat arc just over a hundred paces down the court. Cass was next, hers arced slightly higher than Yellow Hair's and landed a few paces shorter. Traveler unleashed his in an even higher trajectory, and it landed just short of Cass's. Long Pipe launched his in a flatter trajectory, and it landed between Yellow Hair's and Cass's. They looked at the elder with amazement.

The game started with Yellow Hair's stone stopping just under two paces from his lance, as judged by Broadleaf. Next, Long Pipe's distance was just six hands from disc to lance. Cass's disc rolled to a stop and fell on its right side. If it had fallen on the left side, it would have been three hands from her lance. Finally, Traveler rolled his stone and threw his lance. The lance point stuck nearly upright in the court's surface. The stone disc rolled up and stopped, still standing, a hand and a half from the stick.

"As usual, Chief, your chunkey equipment is first rate," Traveler said, just a touch of arrogance in his voice. "Did you want some mint tea for your sweat bath?" he joked, looking over at the younger generation.

"Next time." Cass coolly looked at the sweat lodge set up.

"My fault," said Yellow Hair, "I got too anxious."

"Oh, I think we did pretty well for our first chunkey game. Traveler says they play it all the time in Cahokia. There are other rules and methods, and many different sizes of the discs and sticks. He says even the little children of the important clans play it. I think this Cahokia must be an amazing place. I am beginning to look forward to seeing it," Cass suddenly sounded eager to get to Cahokia. Traveler failed to mention that grown women were not chunkey players in Cahokia.

"As long as I can look on you, I do not care where I am, my woman."

"What if you had the choice between me and your Norway?"

"That is a silly question. There is no chance for us to get to Norway. It is just too far away. Greenland, maybe. But this land is so big, with so many wonders, I am not sure I even want to go there. I understand it is only hills and grass and ice. Here there are trees, at least. That makes it more like Norway. And, of course, you are here. I want to be where you are."

She smiled brightly at him.

While the older men were in the sweat lodge, Cass and Yellow Hair slipped out of their clothes and into the cool stream that flowed by. The cold water nearly took Yellow Hair's breath away. He soon got used to it while he and Cass frolicked for a bit. Eventually, he held on and embraced her. Their bodies made full contact in the cool, spring fed creek. His hardened manhood told her what he had in mind.

Suddenly with two big splashes, the two older men were in the water with them. "I hope you have those drying skins ready. I want to get out now." Traveler looked mischievously at Yellow Hair.

"Yes, Master!" A frustrated Yellow Hair climbed out of the rinsing stream, keeping his back to everybody, and wishing his erection would go away.

The older men grinned at each other. Cass sheepishly looked at the water, her face red as a cardinal flower. She quietly slipped out of the water, quickly wiped the excess water from her athletic body, slipped her loin cloth and shirt back on and said she would go check on the tea. She did not look at Yellow Hair, who still refused to face anyone.

With Cass out of hearing range, Long Pipe walked over and quietly addressed Yellow Hair. "Welcome to the brotherhood of men, son. We are all so blatantly jealous that another one of us might score a fine female prize, we must disrupt at the most inopportune time. Relax. I know that is difficult but take it all in fun as it is intended. You will not die because you did not ejaculate. And the girl will be waiting patiently for the next time. So just put your manhood and your foolish pride aside and be patient. I can promise you that this is something we have all been through, more than once, I am afraid. Traveler loves you as a brother or an uncle would. He only has your best interests in mind. Remember that. It will be important in the near future."

Yellow Hair and Bright Moon/Cass had not been able to find any privacy since that first time, outside of Monongahela Village. Both were frustrated with pent up sexual energy.

"Why is it so important that Cass and I have to wait? Why will no one explain that to me? Everyone seems to know everything except me! What is everyone hiding?"

Traveler came over and joined in. "You should wait because a very powerful man awaits your arrival in Cahokia. He believes, or at least pretends to believe, that you are a messenger from the sky gods. He expects you to be pure and untouched by human flesh if you get my meaning.

"Once he sees you, I need to convince him that you are a man, just like any other. He must come to know that you are not the god that some dreamer claims you to be. Only as an ordinary man are you no threat to his position as Great Sun. That is why I must take you to Cahokia—to demonstrate to him that you are just a lost, ordinary man. Do you understand? If you show up with a pregnant woman in tow, I think he could react in a very bad way. Your life could be in danger."

"How does Bright Moon fit into this? Why is she brought into it? If my life is in danger, hers could be too. What kind of a friend are you? You could have left us alone upriver, and we would be safe. No, you drag us to our deaths in Cahokia. You are being paid for this! You are going to destroy that beautiful woman in there for your own benefit. How much are we worth, Traveler? I cannot believe I fell for your 'friendship' game." His fists knotted, the muscles in his arms rippled.

"Easy now, Yellow Hair. You are reading this wrong. Let me start at the beginning," Traveler started with Far Gazer's great-grandfather. "A prophecy was made that their lineage was directly descended from the gods and charged with building Cahokia into a great city. That the lineage was tied to the Hero Twins and the coming of The Morning Star, who would be re-quickened into Far Gazer's firstborn son. A problem developed in that Far Gazer was having issues producing an heir.

"In stepped the dreamer who 'saw' your arrival on the beach on the eastern shore. The dreamer told Far Gazer that his vision showed him *you* are the messenger who will bring the Son of Morning Star. That means you could be a god, and in Far Gazer's mind a true ruler of Cahokia and the rest of the world, for that matter. You can imagine that Far Gazer is not in favor of some strange, light-skinned boy coming and taking his world away from him. So, he sent me to get you and bring you to Cahokia.

"He will see that you are no god, send you on your way, and probably execute the dreamer for making up the whole thing. I think some trader mentioned you to that dreamer, and suddenly he had a very valuable 'dream' to sell to The Great Sun. Cass coming into the picture was purely by coincidence. She had used herself up mentally in preparing for her fight with Thunder Throat and felt rather useless afterward—until you came into

41

the picture. She asked me to bring her along because she sees a future for the two of you. I am a big softie for a great love story, and it was easy enough to see that you feel the same about her, so I said she could come.

"So, are you going to make my whole plan blow away like smoke and become a hunted refugee by Far Gazer's assassins, endangering you, Cass, and anyone associated with you? By coming along, we must make people think you are my apprentice traveling companion and Cass is my slave. We cannot afford to let anyone think that you and Cass are lovers. Far Gazer will expect you to come in pure. There is no need to mention Stinger, by the way. A baby in Cass's belly would upset Far Gazer. That is why we interrupted you earlier. I hope you can forgive me."

"This is so complicated, and I am not sure I do understand. But you obviously know this Far Gazer better than I do. The thought of anything bad happening to Cass is difficult. I absolutely love her."

"It is good you two did not cross paths before she went to meet Thunder Throat. She would not be deterred from her vision. You may have distracted her enough to cost her life.

"You do understand what you are getting with her, do you not? She killed a man who was considered by many to be the greatest warrior who ever lived, at least in this part of the world. That makes her the greatest warrior that ever lived, man or woman. She killed an adult male mountain lion with a small women's club when she had seen but ten-and-two summers. The point is, that woman means what she says. When she says, 'Build me a lodge,' you better not say 'tomorrow.' Do you understand?"

"I do. I would build her a Great *Norse* Hall with my bare hands if she asked for it."

"Let us go get some of that tea." Long Pipe broke his long silence.

At the fire that night, they heard the story of Cass killing the mountain lion in her own words. Yellow Hair hung on every word.

## CHAPTER 5
# ENTERING ILLINI COUNTRY

J ust before the sun set the following night, the canoe was loaded and ready to journey downriver. They would only be traveling at night until they neared the Grandfather River where they could blend in with the rest of the river traffic.

Before light after their first night downriver from Squirrel Tail Village, they slipped into an obscure creek channel on the south bank. They found a thicket close by to sleep in. They set up strategically placed fall sticks around the canoe so if any animal or human tampered with it, they would be alerted.

Traveler figured they should be far enough away from any dwellings that they should be safe.

All three settled in for a day of sleep. Soon, they would need a guard posted each day.

Around midday, Cass stirred. She had been having a restless dream about dropping Yellow Hair's baby. She looked around and saw no movement, except a pair of gray squirrels chasing one another through the limbs of a large beech tree. She felt moisture between her thighs and panicked. *Oh no, not now! How could this happen? I am traveling with men. I will curse us all! I should have been better prepared.* She moved carefully and silently away from Yellow Hair's heat and started to stand when Traveler stirred. "What is it?" he signed quietly, looking around.

"I must tend to nature," she mouthed and signed. Her eyes darted to the place she sat in the canoe. Her personal bundle was there.

Her glance did not go unnoticed. "Is it your moon?" he mouthed.

She nodded, and he rolled his eyes.

He mouthed again, "Take care of it, and be ready to go after dark."

"What about the woman's curse? I cannot swim all night."

"I do not believe in that superstition. Just be ready after dark," he signed and mouthed at the same time.

"What about him? I do not want to endanger him," she mouthed and signed back.

"He is not superstitious either," he answered for Yellow Hair.

That night as they were preparing to leave, Yellow Hair noted that Cass had gone farther away than normal to take care of her business. "Do you think she is sick? Where can she be? Maybe I should go loo—" Traveler grabbed his arm and shook his head, then motioned him to go to the canoe. "But she does not know this area, she could be lost."

"She would not be lost in Norway. Her moon started that is all. Do not say anything to her. You do not believe any of that superstitious stuff about women and their moon, do you?"

"About a curse, and no contact with men, and so on? Of course not. I have thought about that a lot over my life. The woman is the same person when she is in her moon as when she is not. I cannot see how a little blood is evil. That same blood has something to do with babies, so how can it be evil? I think it is just a time for the women to get away from men for a few days to clear their minds. No, I am not afraid of a little woman's blood."

"Good, I hear her coming, do not say anything,"

Cass casually went to the canoe, set her bag on the floor, grabbed her paddle, and climbed in without saying a word and not making eye contact with either of them. She obviously felt differently about *the curse*.

They moved downriver in silence with a sliver of moon and stars for light. After what he reckoned was five hands of time, Traveler sought out another small brush-choked channel cutting into the south riverbank where they could hide for the day. During the night, they had seen a handful of campfires along the north bank and only one on the south.

When the canoe was hidden, Traveler and Yellow Hair set the noise traps around the canoe while Cass climbed the bank to find shelter. To Yellow Hair's chagrin, she set the men's bags and blankets in one little thicket and her own in another. Her body heat would not keep him company today. He started to go talk to her when Traveler caught his arm. In the dim starlight, Yellow Hair saw Traveler shake his head. Cass was just wandering off to find a private place to take care of her needs.

She found a good place with soft soil and many old leaves. She replaced the dried absorbent moss in the mesh liner she made for her loincloth and dug a hole two hands deep in the soft black soil with her old chert knife. She relieved herself, put the used moss in the hole, filled and packed the soil on top, then covered the place with dried leaves. After she was finished, she returned to the campsite, laid out her sleeping skins, sat down cross-legged facing away from the men, and dug into the bag of venison jerky that Long Pipe had given her.

*At some point, we will need to find a place where we can hunt and cook some food. Our supplies surely will not last the whole journey to Cahokia.*

She looked out across the forested floodplain. It looked like every other floodplain she had ever seen. *I am not far from home yet.* She laid down and drifted into another restless sleep.

Yellow Hair watched Cass with intense curiosity, waiting for her to turn toward him in the dim light and at least wave her hand. She never looked his way. *What is in her mind,* he thought as he tried to get comfortable. He wanted to get to sleep before dawn, but his mind would not relax. Cass and her *curse* kept his mind racing. Finally, in a groggy voice, Traveler said, "Will you relax and go to sleep." It was a statement, not a question.

Several times that day, Yellow Hair woke up. Each time he looked over and saw Traveler deep in sleep, and Cass was an unmoving lump in her little cedar thicket. Each time he fought himself back to sleep.

———

*Cass was standing looking down on Yellow Hair as he slept peacefully on a blanket. She studied his naked body. My perfect man! She tossed her dress aside and carefully kneeled at his hips. She reached out and took his manhood into both her hands. As she did, the limp organ began to respond to her touch. She smiled as it engorged and became rigid in her grip. She looked at his face. His eyes were still closed, but his mouth was bent in a wide smile. She straddled him, guiding his manhood into her. She bent to kiss his smiling lips.*

*Suddenly his face changed. Thunder Throat's painted face filled her eyes. She could smell and taste his fetid breath. He was under her, his huge manhood deep in her. "No!" she cried out and tried to get away. But she was trapped in his powerful arms. He rolled her over, so he was on top of her and began thrusting himself into her mercilessly.*

Cass screamed out and bolted straight up. She was soaked in sweat with her blanket tightly wrapped around her. In her peripheral vision, she saw Yellow Hair start for her. She threw her hand up and told him to stop. "Just a bad dream," she said. "Go back to sleep. I am all right."

Traveler looked on, curious, but did not utter a word before rolling over and drifting back to sleep. Cass was grateful.

Yellow Hair fought to not rush to his woman's side. She was adamant she wanted him to stay away. He struggled to get back to sleep. After spending some time pondering what had haunted her sleep, his eyes closed, and sleep came.

Sometime in the late afternoon, his eyes opened again. Traveler had not moved, but Cass's blankets lay flat in her thicket. *She must be tending to her needs again.* He lay there waiting for her to come back. He heard nothing but birds and a couple of squirrels bounding around on the forest floor. Finally, he got up and decided to track her if he could. At her thicket, he noted she had taken her weapons with her. Her tracks led up the little creek. He retrieved his bow, quiver, and war club and set out on her trail. After a finger of time, he saw a movement ahead. He froze. Soon enough he saw it was Cass returning with a fat turkey slung over her shoulder.

He waited until she got close enough and said quietly, "Are you crazy? We do not know who is around here. We cannot just go out hunting alone. It will be dark soon and we will be on our way. We cannot cook that thing anyway. What were you thinking?"

"Relax, Uncle, I scouted far and wide, and there is no one close on this side of the river. This turkey presented itself to me, so I took it. We do not have enough pemmican and jerky to last the whole trip, so we need to hunt sometime. If you are serious when you say you do not believe in the 'curse,' we can share this bird. I must get this thing cooking." She confidently walked back toward their campsite.

"How? You know the smoke will give us away, right?"

"Watch and learn."

Back at the creek near their campsite, she showed him a place in the channel where floodwaters had undercut a cavernous overhang in the creek bank. She carried dry wood and kindling back into the deepest recess and kindled a small fire. The dry wood produced little smoke, and what there was just hung in the concave ceiling of the overhang. There were exposed roots there that just seemed to absorb the small amount of smoke. Soon she had slices of turkey meat sizzling on sticks.

Traveler stuck his head into the overhang, assessing the situation. "Genius! I am starving."

They ate what they could and packed the rest in tanned rabbit skins. They covered the hot coals with damp dirt and stepped on it until the steam dissipated.

They waited a couple of hands of time before setting out on the river. Traveler briefed them on what to expect. Most of the dwellings and towns were on the north side of the river. The individual farms and small communities were usually friendly, but the chiefs in the bigger villages and towns were aggressive and very unfriendly to most traders. Much fighting had come to this part of the Spirit River, and no one trusted strangers anymore.

They would only travel about five hands of time each night and would hide away on the south side like they did that day. From this point forward, he explained, they would need to have a guard posted at their campsite during the day. They would do that in shifts. He suggested to Yellow Hair that after shaving his facial hair, he should use charcoal mixed with bear grease to darken his hair, face, arms, and legs. "Any of the Illini chiefs who see that yellow hair will want it on a scalp stick, adorning his lodge."

The bear grease mixed with charcoal and mint helped soothe some of the many cuts Yellow Hair's face endured while he was shaving in the twilight. When all was applied, he looked a little like a sickly man with a pox on his face.

During the night while they slipped quietly

down the south side of the Spirit River, they noted a few more clusters of long houses and two palisaded villages on the north side. Late in the night they saw a palisade that appeared half destroyed by fire. A few visible humps of burned and abandoned longhouses could be seen through one burned-out section of the wall. When Traveler had decided it was time to find a hideout for the day, lightning could be seen flashing occasionally on the western horizon.

CHAPTER 6

# CHAPTER 6
# HUNTERS

As the sun approached its midday height, bilious black clouds marched from west to east. Thunderbirds announced their arrival long before they started loosing their lightning arrows at the underground spirits. When the storm front approached, the steady wind from the east got stronger and stronger. It became impossible to sleep.

They decided to pull the canoe up the bank onto the flat ground and tie it to two trees. Then they put on leggings, full hunting shirts and got out water-resistant robes to ward off the coming heavy rain. Finally, they stretched their sleeping skins over the canoe to keep water out. The skins were stretched over the top and weighted along the sides with heavy broken tree limbs.

Just as they were about to hunker down at the base of a massive bur oak, the winds calmed, and an eerie quiet settled in the forest. No birds were chirping, and no squirrels were chasing one another or scolding the intruders. Lightning bolts shot from the dark clouds, and loud thunder rumbled across the hills and the wide river valley. A few large raindrops began to fall, and the wind came hard out of the southwest with renewed strength. Soon branches and limbs began snapping off throughout the forest. The lightning became intense, and rain fell in buckets. Yellow Hair was reminded of the storm that claimed his family.

Suddenly an ungodly roar swept in from the west. They could not see far because of the blowing debris and rain, but the roaring sound swept by their position under the old bur oak just to the west. The terrifying sound of snapping and shearing tree trunks could be heard above the deafening roar of the wind. A few branches and limbs hurled by the big wind landed just to the west of them, and even the big tree they were under suffered some damage. As quickly as it came, the big roar disappeared. But the lightning followed by loud thunderclaps and heavy rain continued. A hand of time later, it started to let up some.

As they started to move and look around at the damaged forest, a great blue-green cloud drifted over the hills toward them. The intense lightning resumed, and the winds reinvigorated one more time. All at once, fist-sized chunks of ice were being hurtled from the clouds and driven by the winds. The big ice chunks pelted the forest for a finger of time, then gave way to smaller ice balls that came in sheets. Their refuge at the base of the big oak tree protected the party from the driving hailstones. The ice balls gradually got smaller and smaller, but not until ice covered most of the ground and lay in small mounds in places. The rain gradually slackened and stopped. Before the sun set, it broke through the cloud cover giving the valley a steamy look as the storm pushed to the northeast.

They had enough light to see that the roaring wind cut a swath through the trees from the top of the first hillside nearly to the south bank of the river and over a hundred paces wide. The trees in the swath were laid down in neat rows as if they had been grass cut with a scythe. They did not lie in the twisted heaps that Traveler had seen after a twisting demon wind traveled through a forest. This was different. He had seen powerful wind gusts before, but nothing like this.

"A hoard of Norse warriors with axes could not

do this!" Yellow Hair waved his arm across the destroyed trees. Cass and Traveler just looked at him.

They went back to the canoe to assess the damage. Tree limbs had fallen close, but the canoe was undamaged, and the skins, though soaked, were still intact. Just a little water had invaded. "We are making a lot of muddy tracks. We better leave and paddle hard as soon as we can tonight." Traveler wanted away from this place.

"Maybe the curse is a silly superstition." Cass worked alongside the men as they were preparing to shove off. "We were huddled together, me and two men, a terrible storm raged, and here you both are—undamaged!"

They all laughed as they started their nightly journey.

That night, they traveled the river under a clear sky and brilliant starlight. If anyone saw them, they were too busy repairing storm damage to do anything about it.

Four days later Yellow Hair had the midday guard shift and was scanning the forest when he caught a movement. Three men were hunting through the trees, apparently assessing the age of deer tracks. He froze in his position fifteen paces from where Cass and Traveler slept peacefully in an ash thicket.

The men were seemingly moving randomly through the trees, but they were following a deer trail. Possibly the same deer that had passed by the fat beech tree Yellow Hair was hiding behind. The hunters wore only breechclouts and moccasins, and each carried bow and had a quiver tied to a waist belt. Their heads were shaved but for a scalp lock on the back right of their heads. The scalp locks were braided and bore a single eagle feather that hung down the back. He could see now that their skin was coated with grease. He guessed them to be about his age. He dared not alert the others because the hunters had gotten too close.

The hunters continued to close in on him until they were just a few paces away. Yellow Hair clung tightly to the opposite side of the tree. Suddenly, the one in front stopped. Yellow Hair could hear air sucking into the man's nostrils as he sniffed the air. Yellow Hair knew the hunter was smelling him.

The hunter motioned for the others to look ahead and around, then nodded slightly in Yellow Hair's general direction. All three raised their bows but did not draw. Yellow Hair waited. They obviously did not know exactly where he was.

The leader inched forward, using his nose as a guide. Yellow Hair could not use his bow without giving away his location.

*When I move, speed is the only thing that will keep me, and the others, alive.*

When the lead hunter was but three paces away and looking at a moccasin track Yellow Hair had left on that side of the tree, he sprang into action. He swung his club around, smashing the hunter's bow, wrapped his arms around the man, and slammed him into his closest friend.

The third was trying to get an aim on Yellow Hair when an arrow from Cass's bow slammed into the hunter's bow just above the man's left hand. It dropped, and the arrow fell to the ground. He grabbed his war club and started for Yellow Hair. Yellow Hair had knocked out the first hunter with a powerful punch to the face and was wrestling with the other.

"Stop!" Cass yelled as the man with his drawn club approached the two writhing bodies on the ground. When the man saw the arrow pointed at his chest, he stopped and glared at her. Traveler was up now, and his arrow was also pointed at the hunter. The hunter's war club dropped at his feet.

Yellow Hair quickly overpowered the man he was wrestling with and had him face down with his hand pinned behind his back. They bound the three men together and wrapped a rope around them, so they were sitting back to back to back, facing out.

Traveler explained that they were not looking for trouble and would not harm them. He said they were just passing through headed upriver to Monongahela Village where this woman was to be married to the war chief's son. The blotchy-faced man was her bodyguard.

Traveler learned the men came from a village two hands of time downriver, and this was their Bear Clan hunting ground. Traveler offered each a piece of jerky and a drink of water. He said he would let them stay the way they were to ensure that his party would be far enough away that the hunting party would not decide to pursue them.

While Traveler and Yellow Hair were tending to the hunters, Cass was busy cutting basswood and cedar bark strips to replace the ropes binding the men. "These are so you do not have to pay my father for the ropes. Is that what you wish, uncle?"

"Yes, that is correct, dear niece."

Yellow Hair was amused at how quickly *his woman* could think.

Yellow Hair noted one of the men leering at Cass's chest while she was bent over replacing the ropes on his feet. By her smirk, he could tell she noted the bulge in the prisoner's breechclout. Yellow Hair bent down and pulled the man's head back by his scalp lock. "My brother, her betrothed, is much bigger than I, and he gets very jealous of anyone making eyes at this one." He nodded toward a smiling Cass.

Traveler talked quietly with the men until it was time to go, then gagged and blindfolded them with strips of rabbit skin. As they shoved off, he told Cass that she would need to hunt some more rabbits in the morning.

# CHAPTER 7
# ILLINI WARRIORS

Two mornings later when Traveler had decided on a good place to put in for the day, Yellow Hair thought he heard an odd sound behind them. He looked back and, in the starlight, saw three canoes with four or five paddlers striking the water a couple of hundred paces back. He drove his paddle into the water and alerted Traveler. The three of them stroked for all they were worth.

At first all three canoes were gaining on them. Then, one started to fade. Soon only one was getting closer. Cass pulled their canoe with all she had. Yellow Hair and Traveler did the same. Traveler began to tire first. He marveled at the strength and stamina Cass was displaying. Their birch-bark canoe had been built to outrun the heavier dugouts. The problem was the canoe behind them was a birch-bark craft as well, although it was a heavier one made for the big river with higher, reinforced ends. Cass and Yellow Hair were able to propel theirs faster because the pursuers carried an extra person, and they sat deeper in the water. Gradually they were able to put a little space between them and their pursuers.

Yellow Hair, Cass, and Traveler managed to get around a bend in time to duck into a small hidden cove. They got their canoe hidden and scrambled up the bank to find cover just as the pursuers rounded the bend. A second bend lay just ahead, causing the lead warrior a moment of hesitation. Looking in their direction in the gray light of early dawn, he obviously saw where the reeds were trampled on the bank where they had scrambled to the top. Before they got into arrow range, the leader called out, "You cannot escape!"

In their tongue, Traveler called back, "What do you want?"

"Your hair!" They pushed their canoe ashore out of bow range and jumped out carrying bows and war clubs.

"Pick your shots carefully but make it quick-those other canoes will be here soon." Traveler only thought he was taking charge. Morning light began to diffuse into the dark forest.

An arrow left Cass's bow. "Not y..." Traveler started to say when a warrior screamed in pain and fell. "As I was saying, nice shot."

"They will wait us out until the others arrive." Yellow Hair jumped up and ran deeper into the woods. A warrior started after him but did not get far before Yellow Hair's arrow bored through his chest. One of the two remaining let out a loud war cry.

"They will be on us soon." Traveler could see Cass draw back her bow. He still could not see the target when she released the arrow. A warrior screamed out as the arrow sliced across his back just below his shoulder blades.

"He should have chosen a bigger tree." Cass calmly watched as the man she wounded lay on the ground writhing in pain when Yellow Hair's arrow plowed into the last one's chest.

"Let's get out of here!" Traveler yelled, but just then, he saw a man running through the trees toward Yellow Hair with his war club raised. Traveler watched Yellow Hair deflect the blow with his own club, duck and drive a big shoulder into the warrior, slamming him against a tree. The man's club fell harmlessly to the ground.

Another started to yell as Cass's war club smashed mercilessly into his chest. He never saw it coming. The other two were closer to her than

Yellow Hair. She blocked a war club, twirled, and slammed her club into his shoulder. She never slowed as she dipped, twisted, and crushed the last one's skull with a powerful swing.

*Remind me to never tangle with her!* Traveler watched Cass fight with amazing speed and skill.

They scrambled to their canoe and drove their paddles into the water as the last four warriors ran to the bank shouting obscenities at them. Soon a couple of arrows rained down near them, but they were quickly out of range. "We still have to find a place to hide for the day." Traveler panted as he continued to paddle feverishly. In a hand of time, they found a likely spot and pulled in. Traveler and Yellow Hair slept first. Cass was still too full of adrenaline to calm down. An unlucky rabbit came close enough for her to stab with an arrow. She had it cooking on one of her smokeless fires when Yellow Hair awoke.

"You are pretty handy with that war club."

"Not so bad yourself. I hope we never have to test each other." She smiled at her man, then looked down. "I really thought I was finished killing people with Thunder Throat." She stared into the distance.

"It seems there is no shortage of enemies in this world."

"What of your world? N...Norway? Are there

enemies there?" Cass turned innocently toward him.

"My people have been at war with somebody, often our own neighbors, as long as anyone can remember. And before that the Bible talks of wars tens of tens of tens of sun cycles past. Men are warriors at heart. I should say some men are warriors at heart, and the ones who are not are forced to join in by the ones who are." There was melancholy in his tone.

"So, it would seem. Do you think we should wake Traveler for some rabbit?" She deftly changed the subject with a coy smile.

"He would only interrupt us again. Yes, better wake him before I disappear into the forest with you." He smiled back, want in his eyes.

---

*TOR FOUND himself walking along a lake high in the hills on his family farm in Norway. A rocky stream flowed from the forest close by and drained into a lake. Bright Moon stepped out of the forest and walked toward him as if floating over the grass to the stream bank. She wore a flowing blue linen dress with white filigree running from the shoulders, down over her firm breasts to the waist. As she approached, she unhooked the dress at her neck, and the entire gown slid down off her sensuous body. Her shiny black hair flowed from her head down her body like a black waterfall all the way to her waist. Her firm breasts protruded from the cascade of raven hair; her dark nipples surrounded by areolas stood straight out. She took his hand, lay down in the grass, and pulled him down on top of her. They made magical love, her pleasure enveloping him until he released his seed.*

Suddenly, he woke up in a birch thicket along the Spirit River. His breechclout was soaked with his sticky seed and pressed against Cass's thigh. As he awoke, she smiled at him and whispered, "Did you have a good dream, my man?"

His face turned red, and he hurriedly got up and went to the stream to bathe, his breechclout still on. She joined him.

———

THE NEXT TIME Traveler was on guard duty, Cass turned to Yellow Hair and gently slid her hand into his breechclout. "You need this, my love." His response was immediate, and it did not take her long to fulfill his need.

He responded by sliding his hand up Cass's thigh and into her loincloth. He remembered what Stinger had taught him about exploring a woman's folds. He could hear her breath catch when he found her moist womanhood. He felt her body accept his touch and tense as he worked his magic. He watched the expression on her face and her fluttering eyes as he probed. Finally, she heaved and convulsed, her eyes rolled back in her head, and her back arched as she squeezed his fingers with all her strength. When she finally relaxed, she looked at him smiling and whispered in a husky, breathless voice, "And I needed that!" They both got up and ran to the stream.

Traveler noted their activity and smiled. *I should have known they would not be able to keep their hands off each other. Too close for too long. I could not keep my hands off her either, under different circumstances.*

Yellow Hair and Cass were not able to refrain from *touching* each other at least once a day whenever Traveler was on guard after that. Their touching soon evolved into passionate coupling. Traveler had the courtesy to move away far enough that they could not see him. Her expressions of pleasure became more vocal as Traveler moved farther away from them.

# CHAPTER 8
# THE GRANDFATHER RIVER

Their luck held when they passed by the bigger Illini villages and towns. It seemed the sky was overcast, raining, or foggy whenever the lights of many fires appeared, indicating a larger village.

*Perhaps guardian spirits truly are watching over us.*

When they neared the confluence of the Spirit River with the Grandfather River, the number of camps, villages, and towns increased, as did river traffic. They had passed the Illini lands and could now travel on the river without fear. It became easy enough to blend in with the large number of canoes going to the big towns along the Grandfather River.

At their last resting spot before they would

make it to the Grandfather River, Traveler told Cass it was time for her to put on her dingy *slave* dress and start acting the part. He had her rub dirt on her face and in her hair, that was now more than a finger long. She rubbed dirt on her arms and dragged a greenbriar vine across them and below her dress on her legs so she would look abused. She beat her arms a few times with a stick and punched her own cheek to raise bruises. Yellow Hair winced as Cass abused her beautiful skin just so he could get into Cahokia without suspicion. It took some convincing from Traveler and her to get him to go along.

The night before they would hit the Grandfather River, Cass moved her sleeping blankets away from Yellow Hair and Traveler again. This time no questions needed to be asked, and the men let her handle her moon in her own way.

Traveler took the rear of the canoe with Yellow Hair up front and a forlorn-looking Cass in the middle. Her paddle would lay hidden next to her in the canoe and only be used in an emergency. Yellow Hair had his hair freshly blackened and all exposed skin darkened. He had learned to shave with his obsidian knife in the dark without cutting himself. Cass had taught him how to chip a fine edge along the blade using the tip of a deer antler tine.

Before reaching the Grandfather River, they crossed over to the north side of the Spirit River so they would not have to negotiate the turbulent waters where the two rivers came together. They were just another canoe in the traffic moving north. Cass and Yellow Hair were in awe of the size and current in the Grandfather River. Traveler told them he expected that it got its name because almost all the rivers in the middle of the world drain into it, so it must be the oldest river, thus it was called the Grandfather River.

While they made their way north, Traveler took care to put in and camp with other traders he knew and trusted or secluded places they could camp alone. The going was slow against the strong current of the Grandfather River, even though they stayed as close to the bank, where the water moved slower. They passed by settlements, villages, and larger towns. Even Traveler was impressed with how much traffic was making its way upriver. *All this traffic on its way to Cahokia. Solstice has passed, and it is another moon before harvest starts. Still two moons before harvest celebration. Why all the traffic? The town is still growing.* He kept his thoughts to himself.

In four days, they passed by a canoe landing with more canoes beached than Cass had ever seen. To the east, many columns of smoke rose into the blue summer sky, but they could not see the town because the riverbank blocked the view.

"Traveler, why are we not stopping?"

"Cahokia is still a few days travel north. This is one of the outlying towns that was once its own center, but soon, if not already, it will owe its allegiance to the rulers in Cahokia. It is obviously still a big town, many clans of mostly planters. They will bring canoe loads of maize, squash, pumpkins, and beans to Cahokia each harvest season in exchange for protection by Cahokia's priests and warriors from evil spirits and raiders."

They passed another of these big landings before steering into a wide creek that entered the Grandfather River from the East. On the west side of the river, they could see a bustling community with what looked like some dirt mounds being built.

# CHAPTER 9
# CAHOKIA

They proceeded up the slow-moving creek fourth in a line of seven canoes going upstream. They met several others coming downstream causing them all to move along in single file. Tall reeds and rushes lined both sides of the creek. In places, channels into areas of open water appeared. Small dugouts and round skin boats occupied by young men, boys, girls, and women were casting nets or spearing fish in the shallow waters. Others were gathering seeds from marsh plants.

Ahead, many more thin columns of gray-blue smoke were rising into the sky than Cass had ever imagined. Soon, a couple of great mounds of dirt became visible. Dust rose from one of them, and a line of people walked up one of the sides, stopped, emptied a pack from their backs, then continued walking down another route. Still others were working up there causing the clouds of dust to rise.

One mound was visible that had a great lodge standing on it with a steep, thatched roof. The tops of a few other thatched roofs told Cass there were other mounds with buildings.

*Cahokia truly is a great city.*

They rounded a bend and before them was, by far, the largest canoe landing Cass had ever seen. In the center were a series of wooden docks with a few large, wide dugouts tied up. A couple of them had yellow suns painted on their bows. Along the bank were tens of tens of canoes of every description. Some were very wide, hollowed out from huge trees. Some birch bark built in the style of Traveler's and others with higher, strongly built ends. Many were small, built for one or two people. Most were the typical dugouts, long and slender. Most lay hauled up on the bank and turned over. Others were just loading and getting ready to depart. Many people had just arrived, some in large groups with many belongings. Some were the small fishing craft they had seen out in the shallows and marshes bringing in their morning catch.

They found an open slot in an area that had what appeared to be mostly trader canoes and pushed theirs onto the bank. "How does anyone remember where they pulled their canoe ashore? Most of them look alike," Yellow Hair pondered.

"A good reason to have one that looks different —in case you have to make a quick getaway." His had a white hand painted on both sides of the prow. A closer look revealed that the trader canoes had one design, or another painted white on them.

When he noted Yellow Hair studying the trader canoes, Traveler said, "The white symbols mean that a canoe carries the power of trade. It is a bad thing to upset the power of trade. That is why traders can go most places without being molested. Many chiefs use that power to spy on their enemies, so we still need to be careful. White is also the color of peace. All traders travel in peace."

Many canoes were in clusters with variously colored wolves, bears, deer, and other symbols painted on them. Those obviously belonged to the various clans and nations.

They emptied the canoe and turned it over, sliding the paddles under it. Before they left that morning, they strategically loaded all their packs, so it looked like Cass was carrying the bulk of their things, but the weight was evenly distributed.

Traveler harshly barked orders at Cass, and she meekly obeyed, her shoulders slumped and a leg dragging ever so slightly like it was injured. Her long, baggy dress effectively disguised her muscular frame. Yellow Hair just followed Traveler's lead because he had not learned enough of the tongue here to fit in. Traveler spoke effortlessly in many tongues and would do all their talking. Cass acted as if she was looking down all the time but was really taking in all the sights. The bustling activity was overwhelming.

One of the most notable things was the huge mound under construction south of the canoe landing. Its base was nearly as large as all of Monongahela Village. It rose to at least the height of two men. This was the mound she had noticed had a throng of people ascending and descending it. Now she could see that they were bringing baskets of earth on their backs to the top and dumping them. Others were spreading the dirt out in a thin layer at the direction of a few other men. The line was continuous all the way to a nearby pit where dirt was being dug up and placed in the baskets. Tens of men and women were carrying the baskets.

A few other mounds were visible from the landing. Just to the south of the lodges, other workers were leveling a large expanse that appeared to be a great plaza. In one part of the big plaza was a chunkey court where a group of men were gathered to play. There were a number of small lodges in the plaza area that were being torn down, and the materials were being carried off to the west. A row of trader booths stood to the west and stretched to the south along the side of the great plaza.

Between the canoe landing and the base of the big mound and spreading to the east and west were many tens of lodges of several designs. Many were in the shape of rectangular longhouses, and many were square, but some were either round or oval like the ones in Monongahela Village. All the lodges had steep thatched roofs. Cass saw none with bark roofs or walls.

"Welcome to Cahokia." Traveler surveyed the changes since he left over four sun cycles past. "The place has certainly grown since last I stood in this spot. Follow me." He led them on a worn path that led through the lodges and west to the long row of trader booths. The booths started along the west side of the plaza just to the south of where a group of men dressed in plain white skirts looked to be laying out a large square.

Traveler waved a hand at the group of men and said, "A new Sun Clan Mound, I would presume."

He found an open booth and ordered Cass to set the packs down. Through a woven door hanging on the west side of the booth was another awning with woven sides that could be lowered. "This will be home for a bit." Then he got into character and ordered Cass to set up their camp. She wearily set about her work, hoping her hanging head disguised the grin on her face.

"Now what?" Yellow Hair was anxious to get the formalities over so he and Bright Moon could get on with their life together.

"First, I have to find a contact to take us before The Great Sun. It may take a few days before we can get in to see him." Traveler led Yellow Hair back to the east side of the booth, stood in the shade, and looked around. "It is getting pretty late, I doubt...looks like we have company."

A group of five warriors approached from the northeast across the great plaza, stirring up dust as they trotted. They all dressed alike and carried strung bows with nocked arrows in their left hands. As they approached and saw no resistance, they put their arrows in quivers that hung on their waist belts and slung the bows over their shoulders. Their right hands then rested on their war clubs.

They slowed, and the leader walked up to Traveler and smiled. "You have been gone a long time, trader. I hope your trip has been fruitful."

"Always good to get back. I hope you saved me

some black drink, warrior." Traveler looked the warrior in the eye.

"Depends on the success of your venture. Your name has not been kindly spoken in certain places of late." The warrior looked at Yellow Hair as if he could not figure him out. "Who is this?"

Yellow Hair could not understand what was being said, but he knew it centered on him now.

"Allow me to introduce you to Yellow Hair, the object of my quest. Yellow Hair, this is my old friend, Raven Wing, chief of The Great Sun's personal protection warriors." Traveler used the words that Yellow Hair would understand. "It appears our wait will not be long."

"The Great Sun wants me to escort you and your companions back to the Sun Temple immediately," Raven Wing said with authority. Inspecting Yellow Hair closely, he turned to Traveler. "What is so special about him? What is this all about, old friend?"

"I was not expecting to be welcomed so quickly. We need to get cleaned up from our long trip. Maybe use a sweat lodge." Traveler tried to buy some time.

"My orders are for immediately. There will be no sweat lodge. You are not going to answer, are you?" Raven Wing looked Traveler hard in the eye.

"I am sorry, Raven Wing, but I am under orders

of secrecy too. Maybe later when this is all cleared up." Traveler looked toward the northeast across the plaza.

He turned and peeked around the door hanging and called harshly, "Cass! Get out here and ready to go!"

She looked down and walked sheepishly to him. The walls of the enclosure had been lowered on three sides, sleeping blankets rolled out, a fire was set up and ready to kindle in the fire pit. She had a tripod set up with a bag full of liquid by the fire pit and had water skins laid out for a trip to the creek for more water.

"I must bring my slave along, Raven Wing. She is not yet familiar with our western tongue. She will get into trouble in my absence. I have to beat her on a regular basis."

Yellow Hair had to look away. *Cass would kill Traveler in a heartbeat if he tried to lay a hand on her.*

"My orders are to bring the woman before The Great Sun as well, Traveler. He is not happy with you in the first place. I recommend you do not make him wait any longer." Though they were friends, Raven Wing's demeanor was cold.

"You are coming with us!" Traveler looked harshly at Cass.

She lowered her head. "Yes, Master."

They started across the plaza. Cass marveled at

all the activity. To the east, on top of a newly built mound, a group of men appeared to be laying out a building on the level top. Three large, straight logs were already standing in place up there. Another group was on each side of a large log, carrying it suspended from straps over their shoulders. They had carried it to the new mound and were starting up the slope. It looked to be a difficult task.

The long line of people carrying baskets of earth up onto the big mound moved continuously like a great, slow-moving snake. From her vantage point she could see that some were leveling the earth from the baskets. If this mound is proportional to the one just finished, it would have to be taller than the trees when completed.

Looking around, she saw a man with a forked stick on the northeast corner of the great plaza. He held the stick out at arm's length and looked through the fork, which stood exactly at his eye level. She followed his line of sight and saw another man ten-tens of paces away. That man held a stick on which one end was painted white. He held it straight up with the white end up and the other on the ground.

The man with the forked stick gave him some sort of hand signal, and the man with the white-ended stick said something to men with hoes and digging tools. They dug a small area of earth from that spot and the man set the white stick in the area they had dug. Another signal from the man with the forked stick, and the men dug up a larger area of earth.

Still others loaded the dirt into baskets and carried it to a depression that had sticks with pieces of string tied near the ground. They dumped their baskets of earth until the strings were just buried. The ground was raked level and the sticks in the depression were removed. They appeared to be finishing the leveling of a large area of the great plaza.

*This plaza will be nearly as big as the palisade wall around Monongahela Village.*

In another part of the plaza where the chunkey court was laid out, the group of men were now playing. The game was being played between two teams. Each team had four men with sticks and one with the disc. All five men from one team lined up with the disc man in the middle. The disc man started first. As he ran toward the release line, the stick throwers all started at once. The disc man rolled the disc, and the stick men hurled their lances in the direction the disc was rolling. When the disc stopped and the sticks stuck into the court around it, an elder came in and carefully noted the distance from the disc to each stick. Next, the other team did the same thing.

Apparently, the team with the smallest total distance won. There was much back-slapping and cheering going on from a small crowd of what appeared from the distance to be well-dressed men and women gathered to watch the game. A handful of children were among them. The disc men put their discs carefully into skin bags with the hair on the inside, apparently to protect the precious discs. The sticks were equally handled with care. The players and spectators mingled for a short while before departing in different directions.

The game finished about the time they reached the Sun Temple Mound northeast of the plaza. The group started up the steps of squared logs set into the ground leading up the mound on the south side.

Once they reached the top of the mound, they crossed a level area on a path paved with crushed shells that led to the Sun Temple, which stood on a second mound atop the first mound. Yellow Hair, Cass, Traveler, and Raven Wing ascended the steps leading up to the Sun Temple's entrance. Raven Wing's men lined up at the base of the upper mound and looked south.

Raven Wing hoped that Traveler's tardiness would not bring bad things to his own life. He had a wife and two children who enjoyed the privileges afforded the Chief of the Sun Temple warriors.

Traveler hoped desperately that he could convince Far Gazer that Yellow Hair was just an ordinary man, lost and far from his home.

Yellow Hair just wanted this meeting over with, so he could enjoy Bright Moon's company.

Cass hoped that this would be the night she would be married, at least in her mind, to Yellow Hair.

They all went through a curtain that led to an uncertain future.

# CHAPTER 10
# THE GREAT SUN

As the small group passed through the door hanging leading into the Sun Temple, Yellow Hair found himself studying the large room lit by torches mounted on the temple's support posts. The posts were connected to long rafters that reached the high-pitched peak of the roof. Gray-black smoke from the torches slid out of the smoke hole at the top in thin streams into a darkening sky. The roof was made of thick thatch supported by many split cross logs lashed to the log rafters. Several cross-beams lent strength to the roof's construction.

Mounted on the supporting wall posts were masks depicting various animals, animal spirits, animal/human spirits, and other entities of the spirit world.

The high-pitched thatch roof was only lightly stained with soot, indicating it was a relatively new building. A central fire pit held only a bed of cold, white ashes. No fire was needed on hot summer days. Yellow Hair was amazed that all the beams, rafters, supports, and crosspieces were lashed together. It appeared to him these people never used treenails.

In the center of the north end of the big room was a raised platform large enough to hold about ten-and-five people. On the raised platform was a raised seat. On the seat was a man elaborately dressed in a blue-dyed doeskin shirt decorated with a beaded sunburst on the chest and spiral symbols on the shoulders. The shirt overlapped a white doeskin breechclout with a red-fringed triangular flap that hung nearly to his knees. A red cloth sash around his waist hugged the shirt to his slim frame. High moccasins of buckskin, dyed blue to match his shirt, decorated with quillwork and colored beads, covered his feet and shins. His long, black hair with just a few gray streaks was pulled back and tied into a bun at the rear of his head. A yellow spirit bundle was tied on the top of his head, and a beaded forelock hung down to his dark eyebrows. Tattoos depicting the sun and geometric-design bands were displayed on his high forehead and temples. White paint in a fork design decorated his black eyes. A spiral tattoo adorned each cheek. Shell earspools depicting human-like gods with long noses were embedded in his ear lobes.

A second man, dressed not quite so elaborately, stood next to him talking quietly when they walked in. That man looked at them quizzically, then turned, descended from the platform, and walked through a curtain into the rear of the temple.

When the four nervous people lined up in front of the platform, the man eyed each one carefully, as if studying their features. Finally, he broke the silence. "Greetings, Traveler, nice of you to stop by. I hope I am not inconveniencing you." After a short pause, he continued. "Raven Wing, you may wait outside the entrance. I will call you when I need you." Raven Wing turned and walked out of the room. "So, who is in charge of introductions here?" His black eyes bored into Traveler.

"Great Sun, to your right of me is Yellow Hair. He is from a far-off land called *Norway,* and his people call themselves *Norse.* Yellow Hair was the only survivor of two great canoes loaded with men, women, and animals that were moving to new lands on this side of the Great Eastern Ocean. Storms destroyed their canoes, and he ended up washed onto a beach in lands controlled by the

Lenape People. He is working with me, learning to become a trader. The woman is my slave whom I acquired by helping the people of Mud Town rebuild in a new location."

"Heh...Heh...Heh. How long have you been working on that story? Do you think for a moment that I do not know who these people are? Yellow Hair here is obviously the object of the dreamer Gray Eye's vision from Eagle Man. The one you went after more than four sun cycles past! Remember? Hardly a boy now, is he? And the woman is the infamous Cass—mankiller. Dangerous company, even for you, Traveler. Why the lie?" Far Gazer was less than friendly.

"Great Sun, perhaps if I tell all of the stories from start to finish, you can better understand. I would have each tell their own story, but these two have not yet mastered the tongue spoken in Cahokia. Perhaps we could start in the morning after"—he indicated the three of them— "we have had a little sleep, some food, and get cleaned up."

"Yes, I have important things to tend to tonight. Your timing is interesting, I must say. Raven Wing will escort you back to your trader lodge and post a guard to keep you there until I am ready to listen to your stories. You will make yourselves presentable before you return. Be prepared to enlighten me as to why a six-moon journey turned into more than four sun cycles." Far Gazer's tone was icy as his dark eyes bore into Traveler.

"Raven Wing!" In an instant, Raven Wing was through the door hanging and advancing with his war club drawn. Three guards followed him in, also with war clubs at the ready. "You will escort these people back to the trader's booth and post a guard over them until I summon you to go get them again. No one is to approach them, and they are to remain in their camp. Provide them with food, water, and other necessities, including clean clothing if they have none of their own." He wrinkled his nose as he addressed Raven Wing as if the others were not even in the room.

"Great Sun, do you think that I have so many enemies that our lives are in danger among the trader booths?"

"You, I have no doubt, have many enemies, but the woman has at least one enemy in our midst, and I will take no chances with this one." He nodded toward Yellow Hair and continued, "You heard my orders, trader. I will say no more, but if you wish I can confine you to a guard lodge."

The walk back across the dark plaza was quiet. No one was in the mood to talk in front of their escort, which was now eight men plus Raven Wing. When they arrived back at the trader's tent, three of the guards went farther down the line of booths. In a finger of time, they returned with a raw buffalo roast, a bag of corn and turkey stew, a bag of corn and blackberry gruel, a basket of corn and blueberry cakes, a bag of sassafras and black-berry tea, and three skins of water.

"At least we will eat well." Traveler raised his voice for the benefit of their guards.

"Traveler, what is this all about? Why the guards?"

Traveler relayed what Far Gazer said. Cass dropped her jaw when he said she had an enemy in the city. "I am guessing someone sympathetic to Thunder Throat caught wind of your exploits and seeks revenge. Perhaps the guards are a good idea."

"In the name of Wolf, will it never end?" She threw up her hands in exasperation. "I just want to get on with my life." She looked longingly at Yellow Hair who was deep in thought.

"This cannot be happening." Yellow Hair finally said. "He wants you to tell our stories in detail...he will take no chances with me...Bright Moon has an unknown enemy around somewhere. I thought we came here to put an end to all the dangers and live our lives. I am not liking it here so far!"

About then, the sounds of many men walking and low voices could be heard all around them. Traveler peeked out and saw that their guard had grown to more than four-tens of warriors. No one would get near them, and he would not be able to sneak away to gather news.

"Traveler, a word with you." Raven Wing walked up on the east side of the booth. "Away from any ears. The Great Sun is taking every precaution to make sure you and your party are not disturbed or molested until he is ready to meet with you. You are all to remain in this camp until that time. My men will be posted far enough away to give you privacy but will be nearly shoulder to shoulder. Far Gazer does not want you or your friends to get the idea that you are free to roam around. Rest assured that no one will approach from any direction. It appears we will have to wait until the harvest celebration to enjoy that black drink."

"Can you tell me why he feels that such a big guard contingent is needed? What is going on?"

"Surely you understand that The Great Sun is less than confident in you, considering your long absence. Your young *friend* has matured into a rather large man for only ten-and-seven summers. He may be concerned that you could find it uncomfortable here and decide to leave. He does not want that to happen. Your canoe, by the way, is no longer where you left it." Raven Wing was unable to look Traveler directly in the eye.

"I do not understand! I did what was asked of me. We knew before I left that it was a difficult quest. I am honestly happy we got here at all. There must be something else. What is it, old friend?"

"Even if I had the answers you are looking for, I would have to say that you are in no position to be asking. But I get only orders. If I do not follow those orders, I probably die. I will tell you that about ten days past, a warrior who seeks revenge against your girlfriend in there, showed up here. He says she assassinated a Great War Chief, and he wants her dead. He offered to fight her in one of our plazas for the entertainment of the people. His name is Black Knife. Does that name mean anything to you?"

"No, it does not. But I have seen her fight, and I think this Black Knife is a fool." Traveler answered coolly. Raven Wing lifted his eyebrows but said nothing. "Oh, and she is not my girlfriend. She is with Yellow Hair—they were made for each other."

"Not your girlfriend? How can that be? You are the master at capturing the girls' hearts."

"To start with, there is the age difference—I could be her father. But as I said, when she and Yellow Hair first laid eyes on each other, both were lost. It was comical to watch them." Traveler shook his head as he smiled. "They were hoping they would be married tonight. If I do not get back in there, it could be too late."

"I have no idea what The Great Sun has planned for her, but I think he plans on having Yellow Hair close to him. Otherwise, I would not have this big of a band of warriors with me. I will leave you now. At first light, some of my men will escort you to the creek to get washed up. I hope you have some cleaner clothes...especially for the woman." Raven Wing turned and disappeared into the darkness.

# CHAPTER 11
# MARRIED

When Traveler stepped back into the tent shelter, he was greeted with the smell of roasting meat, corn cakes, sassafras, mint, and berries. There was the buffalo roast sizzling on a flat rock next to the fire. There was also a single bowl of corn gruel with finger marks in it. Cass and Yellow Hair were sitting side by side in clean sleeveless shirts, he in a clean breechclout, she in a clean loincloth. One corner of the shelter was very wet, and their dirty clothes lay in a heap outside the tent wall.

"The buffalo is there for you. Yellow Hair and I cleaned our bodies with water and sand from the floor. We have shared the corn gruel and will wait for you to eat and go find somewhere to sleep before we lay together. Oh, and I have changed back to my childhood name. Now I am known as *Bright Moon* once again."

"You know that The Great Sun is not finished with Yellow Hair? He can make things very difficult, if not impossible, for you." Traveler took out his knife and sliced off a strip of hot buffalo meat.

"We have waited too long now, Traveler. Bright Moon and I will be together from this night forward. The Great Sun will let us be together. Bright Moon has seen it. No more needs to be said." Yellow Hair's confidence was not lost on Bright Moon. She smiled as he talked.

"Suit yourselves. I will sleep with Raven Wing's warriors who are reserves and not standing watch. Raven Wing told me we are all going to the creek to clean up in the morning and to put clean clothes on. We are basically prisoners." Traveler spoke with distaste in his words and shook his head in disgust.

Yellow Hair looked at Bright Moon's face. "Then we will be happy prisoners." She took his hand into hers.

"I better go find a place to sleep before it gets too noisy in here." Traveler chuckled, finished his tea, took up his sleeping skins and stepped out into the night.

Yellow Hair pulled Bright Moon's face to his and kissed her on the mouth. She returned his kiss as she pulled his shirt up. Quickly they pulled each other's shirts off and laid down on their sides facing each other. She welcomed his strong hand on her breast as he gently kneaded it. Her breathing quickened as they passionately embraced and touched each other. It had been several days since they had last found privacy.

Yellow Hair decided that it was time that Bright Moon learned what it meant to be loved to his maximum ability. Rolling her onto her back, he moved his mouth, slowly kissing his way down her neck and to her firm breast, kissing in concentric circles, working his way to her hardened nipple. He took it into his mouth, suckling and circling it with his flicking tongue. He worked from one dark nipple to the other, bringing her higher and higher into her pleasure place.

Slowly, the urge to move lower took over his ministrations. Going on the teachings of Stinger and conversations he had had with Traveler about pleasing women, Yellow Hair kissed and tongued his way down her muscular stomach. He noted her skin twitching with the light touch of his tongue while her deep moaning urged him on. He found her navel and swirled his tongue around it, sending tingling sensations from there into her waiting loins.

His lips caressed and his tongue explored from

her navel to the line of dark pubic hair just below. He took in her feminine scent and was drawn to it like a bee to nectar. He expelled warm, moist breath into her thick, black pubic hair, sending sensations through her aching womanhood. She pushed herself up to meet his mouth, showing him her desperate need.

She had never known this experience. Bright Star had tried to describe her encounters with Red Hand, but Cass was never interested enough to listen. She never expected a man in her life. Now it was all she could do to contain her wanton lust for this blue-eyed marvel who was showing her what she had been missing.

His tongue found the top of the opening that surrounded her womanhood. As his tongue slithered around her little fleshy mound that had grown larger and harder as it engorged, a lightning bolt of pleasure jolted her. She spread her legs wider and thrust herself into his mouth. His tongue swirled around her fleshy parts before entering her desperate woman hole. She wrapped her legs around his back and pulled while her hand found the back of his head and pulled his face into her.

Her body seemed to explode in convulsive pleasure as contractions of every muscle in her body concentrated into her loins. Finally, the climax came, her back arching. Her whole being was swept into a frenzy of feeling. Rainbow colors filled her tightly closed eyes as every muscle in her body clenched in desperation. Finally, she slowly started to relax, still contracting, and quivering all over.

He felt her relax, but his need was greater than he had ever experienced. He moved up, kissing through her pubic hair and up to her navel again. She cupped her hands over his ears and pulled his face to hers. "I want to feel you in me!" she hoarsely cried out. She found his manhood and guided it to her wet opening.

She whispered into his ear, "Take me husband, I am ready for you! Oh, Yellow Hair, take me! I love you, and I want you!"

He pushed into her, then pulled back slightly and pushed again, feeling her warm flesh surround his throbbing manhood. She moaned and squeezed his manhood with all she had. His thrusts sped up as he pushed harder. She reacted in-kind as both drew nearer and nearer their volcanic climax. She thrust herself onto him each time he pushed. At last, she was again overcome with a diffusion of rainbow-colored light in her tightly closed eyes, and an explosion of convulsive energy in her loins that burst into every part of her body.

Yellow Hair held on as long as he could, but when he felt her body begin to contract, he could not stop himself from an eruption that he thought would never end. Finally, he relaxed on her spent and heaving body. They both took several heartbeats to catch their breath, both their bodies experiencing involuntary small contractions. She hugged him, keeping him on top of her while she felt his softening man organ still inside her. For the first time, she noticed her own feminine scent on his face and could even taste her own salt in her mouth.

Yellow Hair pushed himself up so he could peer into her face. She whispered, "It was worth waiting for you to come into my life, husband. I never thought I would hear myself call someone 'husband.' You made this night more special than I ever dreamed it could be."

"I never want to be apart from you, wife."

# CHAPTER 12
# CLEAN CLOTHES

After that first time, their night was mostly sleepless, but both were dressed, and morning gruel was warmed up when Traveler asked if it was safe to come back into his tent.

Bright Moon laughed aloud. "Traveler will always be welcome in the lodge of Bright Moon, but he would need to bring his own blanket warmer." She gently squeezed Yellow Hair's hand. Yellow Hair was grinning like he had just found a pot full of turquoise stones.

"If there is still time before we are summoned, I have to tell you something Ca...er... uh...Bright Moon. Raven Wing told me that about ten days past, a warrior showed up in the city asking about Cass. He is here to kill you to avenge the murder of a Great War Chief. I presume he is talking about Thunder Throat. He wants to get you to fight him to the death in one of the plazas during the upcoming Harvest Celebration. He said the warrior called himself Black Knife. Does that name mean anything to you?"

She stared at her lap. "Yes, he was one of the Great War Chief's most loyal warriors. Red Hand told me that more than two tens were still loyal to him after the Great War Chief was defeated. He said that he was able to turn most of them, but some fled. He thought they went to join the Haudenosaunee bands to the north.

"Apparently Black Knife came this way. I wonder about Long Spur, Sharpshinned, and Shrike. Red Hand said they were supposedly closely aligned with the war chief and close friends with Black Knife. They may have come with Black Knife to make sure he is successful. I will need to be vigilant."

"Raven Wing's warriors will not let anyone near us for the time being. I do not know how long this protection is to last." Traveler looked at the couple with concern written on his face.

"I can assure you that I will be with you at all times." Yellow Hair had a hard set to his strong jaw.

"Perhaps The Great Sun will protect the wife of

Yellow Hair." Bright Moon chuckled. "If they are as incompetent as other Black Bear warriors I have encountered, they are not much to worry about."

"The danger of being a mankiller is that there is always one out there who thinks he can best you. Unless something changes, you will always have *one more enemy* I fear." Traveler's expression had not changed.

"Maybe that is why Wolf promised me no future."

"Enough!" Yellow Hair chimed it. "This is the first day of our marriage. I will not have it spoiled by sadness and worry. It is a day to rejoice and be happy. Come, eat up. We will take the future as it presents itself."

"To a long marriage." Traveler lifted his cup, and they all joined in.

———

A FINGER OF TIME LATER, Raven Wing called from outside the tent to ask if they were ready. He formed a squad to escort them to a creek to bathe. They carried fresh clothing for the meeting with The Great Sun.

At the creek, they washed with crushed soap-weed and rinsed in clean water. Bright Moon noticed a little soreness and burning sensation as she washed her woman parts. A smile crossed her face as she thought of the way her *husband* introduced her to marriage. *Sure, we coupled a few times before we arrived in Cahokia, but last night was a whole new experience!*

She put on the ceremonial doeskin dress that Corn Stalk had given her before leaving Mononga-hela Village. It was lightly tanned and had cattail heads and leaves painted black along the bottom just above the fringed hem. The dress came to mid-calf and was tied around the waist with a soft, blue-dyed buckskin sash. Built into the sash was a loop for the sheath that held her obsidian knife. Her always present war club hung on a hook by her right hip. The dress was sleeveless with fringe around the armholes. The shoulders were decorated with porcupine quill chevrons and bead crosses, each leg in the color depicting one of the sacred directions. Her clean hair, now almost two fingers long, had been rubbed with a small amount of bear grease mixed with mint and was pulled down evenly around her head and held in place with a beaded headband. Four honeysuckle flowers were tied around the headband. She looked ravishing to Yellow Hair.

Yellow Hair had the ceremonial shirt that Painted Turtle had given him. It was made of fringed buckskin tanned to a soft light brown color and decorated with dyed turtles and beaded chevrons. A buckskin belt tied the mid-thigh length shirt around his waist. From it hung a beaded sheath for his knife and his war club. His buckskin breechclout was cleaned and newly oiled with bear grease mixed with mint. He wore the ceremonial moccasins Painted Turtle had given him with fringe around the ankle high hem and quill chevrons on the top of the foot. His cleaned, greased, and minted yellow hair was plaited into a single braid and hung to the middle of his back and was tied off with a plain buckskin thong. His face was freshly shaved. Three eagle feathers were entwined in his hair indicating his success in battle. Bright Moon thought he looked like a regal war chief. His skin had become tanned but was a lighter tone than anyone else's.

Traveler wore a plain, brown tanned buckskin trader's shirt, a buckskin belt, and a clean breechclout. His moccasins were plain and brown as well. A shell gorget depicting a river in a forest hung on a rawhide thong around his neck. His gray-streaked middle-of-the-back length hair was cleaned, greased, and tied loosely behind his ears with a thin buckskin thong.

# CHAPTER 13
# THE SUN TEMPLE

With their warrior escort, they walked toward Sun Temple Mound from the banks of Cahokia Creek. As they wound their way through the lodges, every man, woman, child, and dog stopped what they were doing and stared at the procession. In the distance, Bright Moon saw a man dressed in a dark breechclout and nearly black vest. He stared intently and never took his eyes off her. She stared back at his ugly face.

*That must be Black Knife. He looks full of hate. Wolf, will I have to confront every man who hates women? Please end it,* she pleaded.

Just as they were about to turn to the east, three more men of similar description joined the first. She looked straight up, then glanced at

Yellow Hair who was oblivious to the men she had seen. His attention was on the throng of people carrying dirt to the big mound under construction.

Traveler noted that many of the old-style lodges with post and wall construction had been replaced with the newer trench wall type. Far Gazer's father and his Council had determined the trench wall method better served the sky gods, so all new buildings would be made this way, and as soon as practical, all old buildings would be torn down and replaced with the new kind. Conveniently, the new wall construction required fewer trees to be cut down and transported into the growing city.

Over the past twenty sun cycles, many of the old buildings had been replaced. More remarkable to him was the sheer number of new lodges there were. The city had grown tremendously in the four sun cycles he had been in the east chasing after Yellow Hair. It amazed him that Far Gazer's family had gained so much influence. Each generation had strengthened its hold on the power clans, and now, everything Far Gazer had planned was coming to pass. He had everyone from the lowliest farmer to the high priests believing he was related to the sky gods and getting divine instructions from them.

*How long can he fool them?* As he looked around,

he was amazed to see so many people working so hard to make one man a *god*.

Soon enough they stood before Far Gazer. Yellow Hair and Bright Moon stood on Traveler's left side arm-in-arm in a show of matrimonial unity.

Far Gazer was dressed in a green doeskin shirt decorated like the blue one he had on the night before, along with the white breechclout and triangular skirt. His demeanor was much more pleasant and positive. A man dressed similar to Far Gazer stood to his right and another man of importance stood on his left. "Welcome guests of The Great Sun. Allow me to introduce Smoke Master of the Sun Clan, second heir to The Great Sun of Cahokia and my younger brother." He indicated the man on his right. He then indicated the man on his left. "This is Sun Seer, High Priest of the Sun Temple. The man standing beside Traveler is Gray Eye, the dreamer who foretold the arrival of Yellow Hair." Traveler noted that the dreamer had his vision after a trader mentioned Yellow Hair's appearance on that beach near Willet Village, but Far Gazer failed to mention that detail.

"Traveler, it will please you to know that last night, shortly after our...discussion here in this temple, a male heir was born to me. His childhood name is *Star,* and my priests take the arrival of this yellow-haired man as a sign from the sky gods that he will be a worthy ruler one day. The prophecy of a male heir born in the Month of Ripening Corn has come to pass. When he is an adult, Morning Star himself will inhabit his body. I had not understood that the sky gods had planned your arrival with the birth of my son. Now it has become clear to me that things have happened as they were meant to.

"Now, I want to hear every detail of your stories, especially about our yellow-haired friend here. The woman's story will come last."

"I am pleased that after all this time, an heir has been brought to you. I am sure he will be a great leader." Traveler started talking, though he wondered at the timing. It took him nearly two hands of time to tell the story up to the time he finally met Yellow Hair. He left out the parts about his liaisons with the Head Matrons of Sun Town and Monongahela Villages.

Then he took another hand of time carefully explaining how Yellow Hair got to that point. By that time, everyone was tired of standing, thirsty, and hungry. They retired to a sunshade in the small plaza outside the temple and sat on woven cattail leaf mats while servants brought food and drinks to everyone. The highly decorated Tree of

Life stood just to the east and rose higher than the temple's roof.

Traveler did his best to convey Yellow Hair's religion and beliefs while they ate. The high priest looked on in scorn when Yellow Hair's belief in a single god who controls all things was brought up. But when he understood the conflict between the god and a single archenemy, the devil, he began to nod his head as he listened.

"Order and chaos—The Good Son and the Evil Twin, The Hero Twins, it all makes sense." The priest began to nod his approval. Yellow Hair only understood an occasional word and just took it that Traveler was conveying the ideas correctly.

They stayed outside for the afternoon as Traveler completed the story of how he and Yellow Hair found their way to the Spirit Water River. He spent some time explaining the history of how Thunder Throat came to power and destroyed Bright Moon's village and how she was visited by Wolf/First Man. He told the story of her encounter with Thunder Throat. Then came their adventures down the Spirit River and finally their arrival in Cahokia. At last, he disclosed the marriage between Bright Moon and Yellow Hair in the trader booth after the meeting with Far Gazer the previous night.

"Ask if he knows about this Black Knife." Bright

Moon's nervous eyes and shaky voice betrayed her nervousness in the presence of The Great Sun.

"Great Sun, the maid, Bright Moon, wishes to know what there is to tell about this warrior, Black Knife, who seeks revenge against her."

Far Gazer's eyes perked up and peered into her face. After several heartbeats, he looked her in the eye. "The warrior tells a different version. In his, the maiden witched the Great War Chief and ambushed him in the forest at night. He said you would show up here acting the part of a helpless maiden and beg for help in protecting you. Are you a helpless maiden begging for protection? Is that why you cling to Yellow Hair?"

After Traveler finished interpreting, Bright Moon bristled. She stood up, taking care to flex her powerful legs, looked him directly in the eye, and spoke her best Cahokian tongue. "Great Sun of Cahokia, Bright Moon sees helpless?" Her best was still not very good.

Far Gazer smiled and said, "No, indeed, Bright Moon does not *sees* helpless. I understand this warrior wants to fight Bright Moon in open combat in one of our plazas during the Harvest Celebrations. Other than it being interesting, I have no notion of being a part of any such spectacle. I am confident the maiden can take care of herself, but this Black Knife is a forked tongued snake, and I wish to give him no audience in my city.

"I fear, however, that if no action is taken, he will find his way to her at some point. She obviously has a relationship with our good Yellow Hair here, and I can see that any harm that comes to her also comes to him. I will think of a solution. Gray Eye, what is your opinion of what you have heard to this point?"

"Great Sun, my dream from Eagle Man has been born out. He identified Yellow Hair as the messenger who would bring The Son of Morning Star among us. It is now obvious that he is, indeed, a messenger from the sky gods and is to sit at your right side giving you counsel on the affairs of Cahokia and all you control. Eagle Man never mentioned anything of this maiden. And yet, she claims to have been in contact with First Man himself. That is important, I think. Perhaps Eagle Man will visit me again to make things clear." Gray Eye tried to sound confident and important.

"Sun Seer, what have you to say?" Far Gazer turned to the priest.

"It is all very confusing. *First Man*, or *Eagle Man*, or both, maybe have steered these two together, but for what purpose? I must meditate on that." The priest assumed a haughty demeanor.

Smoke Master got into the conversation. "Our

grandfather said that divinity runs in OUR veins, not those of strangers from far-off places. The sky gods are to hold council with US, no one else. I think this whole thing is folly. Far Gazer, you are Great Sun, I am Second, at least until your son is ready to assume his rightful place. These people are all outsiders. This Yellow Hair ended up here purely by some strange accident. He knows nothing of the Sky World or our sky gods. He talks of only one god. How can that be? What counsel can he give? And the maiden has been a witch, a mankiller, a murderer. What counsel can she give? Why is she even here? And Traveler is just a wandering trader. Why would we listen to him? We are the ones related to the gods here. Why should we listen to any mortal men? Let Sun Seer conduct a séance with us for counsel if you wish. But do not put trust in these outsiders. I say we hand the maiden over to the eastern warrior and let justice be done. Yellow Hair should seek out his own people any way he can, and this trader should ply his craft on the rivers. Let our Sun Clan run Cahokia, big brother. This is what I have to say."

"Your words contain truth, my brother. But our father told me to seek counsel from wise men. These *outsiders*, as you call them, have done wondrous things and may offer valuable counsel. This day has been long. I have many things to consider. Traveler, we will make the same arrangements as last night. But you will have two trader booths tonight so that our newlyweds here can have their privacy. Be prepared to come back tomorrow. Raven Wing!" Far Gazer called for his guard at last. He was there with three other guards in just a few heartbeats. "Escort these three back to the traders' booths and surround two tonight so that Yellow Hair has his privacy."

"Great Sun, my men have reported to me that the four warriors have left Cahokia. They said Black Knife told them he and his men were going someplace friendlier, perhaps the lands of the Caddo People. Their canoe was last seen going south on the Grandfather River. Shall I post fewer warriors?" Raven Wing stood stoically at attention.

"If they are truly gone, there is no need for any guards. Let your men return to their lodges but be ready in case this Black Knife returns."

Raven Wing walked with Traveler, Bright Moon, and Yellow Hair back to the trader booths and chatted about many things. Of particular interest to Traveler was how, suddenly, after fourteen sun cycles and who knows how many maidens, Far Gazer fathered a male child. Predictably Raven Wing had no idea what might have happened. "I have no need to know about The Great Sun's personal life or his plans. My function is to ensure his safety and follow his orders, nothing more. I will not speculate on what has happened while he is out of my vision, nor will I engage in predicting what actions he may or may not take." Raven Wing's tone was one of absolute loyalty to Far Gazer.

# CHAPTER 14

# A PLOT

S moke Master walked with Gray Eye back to his lodge east of the great plaza and just east of the Shell Clan Temple. They did not notice the four shadowy figures following them. The conversation was friendly all the way from Sun Temple Mound.

After the two men rolled out of Gray Eye's sleeping skins, the tone changed. "You will have a visit from Eagle Man tonight. He will tell you that Yellow Hair has fulfilled his role in bringing an heir to Far Gazer. Tell Far Gazer that Eagle Man now wants to see Yellow Hair sacrificed and buried with great honor so that his souls can return to the Sky World and his temporary body lies in great honor in a special mound in Cahokia. The woman with Yellow Hair will also be sacrificed and put in the same grave as Yellow Hair's protector until his soul reaches the Sky World. This will be seen as a great gift to the sky gods. I will be back in the morning to escort you back to the Sun Temple with your new revelation from Eagle Man. Is that clear?"

"How can I just make up a lie like that? It makes no sense. I have had no time to purify my body and souls. He would never believe Eagle Man just showed himself to me, in my lodge, without the required rituals. I am amazed that he ever fell for the Eagle Man dream all those sun cycles past."

"He believed it because he wanted to believe it. He now has confidence in you and your dreams. He will do as your *dream* dictates. Do it, or you will not see another sunset." Smoke Master's dark eyes confirmed his threat.

Gray Eye hung his head and quietly said, "I will make it sound good." Smoke Master left Gray Eye's lodge and started back to the Sun Clan's big lodge, confident his secret plan would ensure he would soon be The Great Sun.

———

BLACK KNIFE LOOKED at Sharpshinned and said, "You and Long Spur go in there and find out where the trader and the woman are staying. After he tells you, slit his throat. Shrike and I will be posted out here and warn you if anyone approaches." The sun was setting when Sharpshinned and Long Spur reached Gray Eye's lodge.

Smoke Master was nearly halfway to the Sun Clan Lodge when he decided to go back and tell Gray Eye he would receive a handsome reward for his new dream revelation. He would have the option of choosing his own reward.

*Perhaps the threat was a bit harsh. After all, Gray Eye has served Far Gazer as only a good man can for the last couple sun cycles and me for as long as I have known him. I really do not wish to lose his tender touch.*

As he was nearing Gray Eye's lodge, out of the shadows, two men grabbed his arms and stuffed a rag in his mouth. They quickly shuffled him into the lodge where Sharpshinned had killed Gray Eye. He and Long Spur were loading several of Gray Eye's painted shell gorgets into a rough cloth bag. Gray Eye lay naked on the floor by the hearth in a pool of blood.

Smoke Master struggled to get free of his captors but was not strong enough.

"Did he tell you?" Black Knife glared at Sharpshinned as he held a knife against Smoke Master's ribs.

"He said they are in the trader booths."

"We know that much, fool. Which one?"

"He said he did not know." Sharpshinned shrugged his shoulders. "But I could not just let him go, so I killed him as you instructed. Surely that one knows."

"This is a high-ranked man. Maybe we should ransom him." Shrike's voice reflected his anticipation of more blood.

"We cannot ransom him." Black Knife twitched nervously. "He is Smoke Master, second only to The Great Sun. Whatever we do, it needs to be quick. That one is starting to smell. Find a blanket to throw over him." He nodded toward Gray Eye's corpse laying on the floor. Flies had discovered the fresh blood and were swarming and lapping up the treat, even as darkness filled the room.

*Good thing it is dark out. Sharpshinned has fresh blood all over his arm and shirt, even on his leggings.*

"Tell us what booth the trader and the woman are in!" Black Knife told Smoke Master in his best Cahokian, while removing the rag from his mouth.

"I-I will show you if y-you let me l-live. I want them d-dead too. I can pay you well."

"No tricks?"

"None. I want them dead as much as you do. I will lead you to them. After it is done, we will arrange a place where I can meet you and pay you. Then you can be gone, and no one needs to know who killed them. Thinking you had left the city;

Far Gazer has dismissed the guards protecting the trader and his party." Smoke Master's air had become conspiratorial.

"I will stay with you until we have our payment in hand. What do you have in mind?"

"What do you want? I have access to many things." Smoke Master's eagerness told Black Knife he had a willing accomplice.

*Gray Eye is out of my way. I no longer need worry about him telling Far Gazer that the Yellow Hair dream was my concoction. Astounding that Traveler found a white-skinned man with yellow hair. He must be one of those foreigners far in the northeast, but how Traveler found him is beyond amazing. Leaking the story out about Far Gazer sending Traveler to the eastern ocean to find a messenger from the gods was brilliant. When nothing came of it and Traveler returned empty-handed, or not at all, Far Gazer would have been shamed, and I would have been named Great Sun. Traveler finding Yellow Hair and bringing him back here just when the boy was born is bad luck. And whoever started that rumor that a trader told Gray Eye about the yellow hair nearly ruined my whole plot. Thankfully a friend silenced that trader, and Far Gazer only believed Gray Eye. But now my luck has changed, and Gray Eye can no longer betray me. Next will be the trader and his company. Maybe I should have them take care of Far Gazer as well. Then I will be*

*The Great Sun, and Star will be raised as my son, as he should be.*

"You have turquoise, obsidian, jet, rose quartz?" Black Knife was already counting his riches.

"All you want...and copper if you like," Smoke Master was making his own plans.

"Let us get on with it then. I want the woman." Shrike had his own agenda.

"Not if I get her first." Long Spur growled.

"The woman is mine! No one else touches her until I am finished! Is that understood?" Black Knife left no room for discussion.

"Yes, War Chief." Long Spur and Shrike were suddenly subservient.

"Not yet," Smoke Master interrupted. "Let the evening activities die down. Wait until everyone goes to sleep. It will be easier to get in there. Kill the two men first, then do what you want with the woman, she is of no importance to me. But if you want to use her, you had better just take her with you. With three bodies around the city, Raven Wing's warriors will be out hunting as soon as they are found. You should get as far away as you can before you play your games with her."

"You have a devious mind, Smoke Master. Maybe you should come with us." Black Knife had a hint of admiration in his voice.

Smoke Master laughed and shook his head.

A hand of time after they heard the last voices die out, they slipped silently out of Gray Eye's lodge, making sure to brush their tracks away with a turkey wing from Gray Eye's lodge. They quietly crossed the empty plaza and neared the trader booths. The booths were all located on the west side and south of center, along the plaza. Their path across the plaza took them far enough from any occupied lodges so that no dogs were alerted and set to barking.

Toward the north end of the line of trader booths Smoke Master stopped them and pointed out which two Traveler, Yellow Hair, and the woman occupied. Shrike and Long Spur volunteered to go after Yellow Hair and Bright Moon, while Sharpshinned would take the trader. Black Knife and Smoke Master would keep watch at the edge of the plaza just outside the trader booths. "Kill the men and bring the woman to me unharmed." Black Knife's orders were barely a whisper.

# CHAPTER 15
# ASSASSINS

Yellow Hair slid off Bright Moon after their third frantic coupling and held her gently so she would fall asleep in his arms. Except he fell asleep almost instantly while she lay awake.

*Just six moons past, I did not think my world would last beyond a sunny afternoon on Rock Ridge along the Spirit Water River. My future looked black. Now, here I am lying next to a man I want to live with forever and looking forward to every heartbeat I spend in his company. Amazing how life changes. I hope that Bright Star finds her new life with Red Hand as pleasing as mine is with Yellow Hair.*

She re-lived the moment she first laid eyes on Yellow Hair and every experience they had together since that day at the Monongahela Village canoe landing.

*What was that noise?*

Her senses went into high alert. She focused her eyes to the darkness in the tent enclosure, picking up the soft, orange glow of the embers in the fire pit. She slid her hand under her sleeping skin and wrapped her hand around the antler handle of the obsidian knife she always kept close by. Silently she sprung up and held a hand over Yellow Hair's mouth to quiet him while he awoke. A finger held against his lips told him not to utter a sound. She sensed, as much as she saw, a figure sliding under the tent awning at the west end of their enclosure. She had her knife against the intruder's throat before he figured out where anyone was in the tent. Long Spur hurried back to Black Knife to alert him they had been discovered. It never crossed his mind that he might help Shrike in the tent with Yellow Hair and the woman.

"What is going on?" Yellow Hair's sleepy voice interrupted the silence.

"Traveler!" Bright Moon tried to alert her friend.

That gave Traveler the warning he needed, and he rolled away just in time to avoid Sharp-shinned's blade driving into his belly. As it was, the knife sliced through his sleeping skin and stuck in the packed ground. Traveler was up and able to kick the intruder in the ribs, driving the air out of the man. He pounced on him and punched him hard enough behind the ear to render the intruder unconscious. He found some straps in his bags and bound the man's hands, arms, and legs.

Yellow Hair and Bright Moon had the other man similarly bound and asked him where the others were. He refused to answer. Yellow Hair's fist in his gut changed his mind, and he gasped that they were with Smoke Master on the plaza side of the wall, between coughs.

Bright Moon grabbed her war club and slipped out into the dim starlight. She saw three figures slinking across the plaza toward the southeast and set out after them.

Looking back, Long Spur turned to confront her. She came on so fast and strong that she deflected his knife hand away with hers while driving her war club into his gut. He crumpled to the ground desperately trying to catch his breath.

The two remaining figures had no inkling how fast their pursuer could run. Suddenly, hearing her bare footsteps closing in on them as they crossed the chunkey court, Black Knife turned to face her. She quickly advanced on him, war club in one hand, knife in the other. Although she had grabbed her war club, she had no time to consider getting dressed.

She could see that the two were splitting up.

Shouts came from the bigger man. She saw his arm draw back and suddenly the smaller figure stumbled and fell. He scrambled to his feet and continued, but at a slower, awkward pace.

In the dim light afforded by the starlit night, Black Knife was astonished to see the speed with which a naked female was closing on him. He drew a second knife back to throw at her. Suddenly his pursuer changed course and was no longer in his aim. A heartbeat later, his knee buckled, and he went down on it. He clumsily turned to look where she was when her club came down hard on his right shoulder, breaking bones and causing excruciating pain.

Bright Moon looked around, but the other figure had vanished into the darkness. Black Knife lay moaning on the ground trying to support his broken shoulder with his other hand. She kneeled behind him, held the knife to his throat, and said calmly, "Care to tell me who was with you?"

"It was Smoke Master. He wanted to pay me to kill the trader and Yellow Hair. He said I could have you." He moaned, gasping for breath in anguish. "I need a healer."

She heard voices and knew people were advancing from the west. "Are you all right, Bright Moon?" she heard Traveler shout from many paces away. Yellow Hair jogged up and handed her the doeskin dress to slip on before the others arrived. He had slipped on his breechclout and brought the dress for her.

"Fine!" she called back.

"You are full of surprises...I never heard the intruder. How did you?" Yellow Hair held her tight against his side.

"Pena sneaked up on Cass many times while she was sleeping—until Cass learned to listen to sounds in the darkness, even while sleeping." Her voice was so nonchalant, he could not question her sincerity. Her panting was almost under control.

"Thank you for the warning." Traveler slapped Yellow Hair on the back.

"Thank her, she's the one with the owl ears and cat moves." Yellow Hair stood shaking his head at the skills demonstrated by his wife.

"That one says Smoke Master is responsible for all this. He was going to pay them for killing you two." Bright Moon pointed to the crumpled figure on the ground, just as several more people came up from the west, including four men escorting the bound prisoners Sharpshinned, Long Spur, and Shrike. "I am glad you are unhurt, Traveler."

"Not exactly, I think I broke my hand on the back of his skull." He pointed to Sharpshinned.

"Black Knife said they were to kill Traveler and

me. What about you?" Yellow Hair gave Bright Moon a worried look.

"I was part of their pay for killing you. I guess they got more pay than they expected." Bright Moon joked, still shaking from the excitement.

Just then, they heard footsteps running toward them and the noises said they were armed warriors. Everyone circled around the prisoners. Black Knife had passed out from the pain in his shoulder after vomiting everything in his stomach.

"What is this commotion all about?" Raven Wing demanded as he came jogging up, war club in his right hand.

"All is quiet now, Raven Wing, but it seems we were visited by these assassins. We will let you question these men and do what you wish with them. We are all available to answer your questions as well." Traveler stood tall and looked into Raven Wing's dark eyes in the dim light of the quarter moon.

"You always seem to be the spokesperson, and always in the middle of any trouble." Raven Wing's tone was filled with suspicion as he glared back at Traveler.

"Traveler," Bright Moon interrupted, "make sure he sees the fresh blood all over Sharpshinned here. That blood did not come from any of us. He needs to find out where else these men have been tonight."

Traveler conveyed that to Raven Wing. "We already know what they have been up to tonight. Smoke Master reported that. He is severely wounded and has lost a lot of blood himself. Sun Seer and a healer are with him now."

# CHAPTER 16
# TRIAL

ate the next afternoon, Traveler, Yellow Hair, Bright Moon, Long Spur, Sharp-shinned, and Shrike stood before the Sun Clan Council of Elders. Black Knife was carried in on a litter. Sun Clan Head Matron, Walks in Moonlight, presided. "Tell us what you know of these warriors, Bright Moon. They came here from your lands." The woman dressed in a green elegant, beaded dress that shimmered in the flickering torchlight sat stone-faced on the raised dais while an interpreter spoke to Bright Moon.

"I only know of them by reputation, Head Matron. They were reportedly loyal to the Great War Chief, Thunder Throat, who was responsible for much torture and many deaths among my people. It was reported to me that after I helped the people of Black Bear Village end his rule, a few who were loyal to him fled. No one knew where they went. I never saw any of them until I heard Raven Wing mention their names. I recognized the names and told him what I knew of them. Then, yesterday as we were moving from the creek to Sun Temple, I saw them in the crowd staring at me. Far Gazer said that Black Knife reported that I had ambushed the Great War Chief and killed him in the dark. That was not true. I fought him in a fair fight on a sunny afternoon with war clubs." Bright Moon's demeanor was confident and portrayed honesty.

"You are saying that you defeated a Great War Chief with just a war club? I find that hard to believe. But that is not why we are here. What happened in that trader booth that you were allegedly able to overpower these men?" Walks in Moonlight questioned her. The woman's mannerisms said she believed Bright Moon was guilty of something.

"I was lying awake and happened to hear the slight scrape of flesh on sand. I was able to adjust my eyes to the dim light given off by the coals in the firepit and get up silently while Shrike, there, tried to slide under the tent wall. I put my blade to his throat before he knew I was there. Then I yelled out to warn Traveler that someone might be coming after him. There was only one in our tent, and I knew there were four of them," Bright Moon answered calmly.

"And how did you come to stop the ones called Long Spur and Black Knife. He claims you are a witch, a serious charge."

"Shrike told us Black Knife was on the plaza standing guard. I stuck my head out and saw them scurrying southeast across the plaza. I grabbed my club and went after them. I think I caught up quicker than they expected. Long Spur turned to stop me, but I slammed my club into his gut before he knew what hit him. He barely slowed me down. Black Knife turned to challenge me while the other one fled. Before he got away, Black Knife threw a knife at the one fleeing. Apparently, it sliced into his side. I did not see who it was. I saw that Black Knife was trying to stop me by throwing a knife at me, so I faked one direction, turned, and slid low to where I could damage his knee with my club. Before he could recover, I broke his shoulder."

"First, why did you go after Black Knife and not your husband? Second, why did you go after him naked?" The Great Chief pushed, disdain in her voice.

"I was just acting on instinct, I guess. I am not used to anyone else fighting for me yet. That will take some getting used to." Bright Moon's honesty was unmistakable.

"Yellow Hair, do you have anything to say about why you let your wife do the fighting? Should you not be the one defending her?" Walks in Moonlight turned to Yellow Hair while the interpreter spoke.

"Bright Moon was witness to her mother's horrible death. During that catastrophe she made a vow that she would avenge her parents' murder and the destruction of her village. To do so she would need to train herself to be a great warrior. She did that. Her instincts and abilities are beyond mine. I would have gladly gone after Black Knife, but she was in pursuit before I even knew where he was. I got there as quickly as I could, but she already had him subdued by then."

"Trader, do you agree with what has been said here?" Walks in Moonlight turned her attention to Traveler.

"Yes, I do, Head Matron."

"Do you believe Bright Moon is a witch?" The Sun Clan Matron was obviously trying to accuse his friend of some nefarious activity as she looked to the council members.

"No, she is no witch, Head Matron. She is an extremely determined and competent young woman who has gained a special set of skills for a woman. She is also sensitive and loving. No, she is no witch."

"Bright Moon, you have been accused of witchcraft. What is your defense to this charge? Keep in mind that the charges stem from your homelands and the actions you took last night." Walks in Moonlight kept pressing.

"Great Chief, as Yellow Hair said, I spent nine sun cycles preparing my mind, my body, and my souls to fight and defeat one man. The man who raped and mutilated my mother and father, along with many others. To get him to fight me alone, I used some trickery where I pretended to be a witch. I did not use any poisons or non-human powers to do that. Just a costume of crow and cardinal feathers. And because I defeated that man does not mean that I no longer have the fighting skills and reflexes I had to learn to fight him. By the gods, I wish I no longer had the need for those skills. But enemies keep showing up that require me to defend myself or someone I love." She indicated Yellow Hair and Traveler.

"All right, you can fight. Do you know why these men had Smoke Master with them last night?" Walks in Moonlight softened her tone a bit.

"All I know is what Black Knife said—that Smoke Master offered to pay him for killing Yellow

Hair and Traveler. I was to be taken alive as part of the payment. Given what I have heard about Black Knife, I do not know if he speaks the truth or not. He certainly lied when he called me a witch."

Walks in Moonlight looked to Sharpshinned and, through the interpreter, asked if he had anything to say in their defense. "All we ever wanted was this murdering witch, Great Chief. It all went wrong because of her witchcraft." He looked at Bright Moon with disdain while he talked.

"She caused you to kill the Dreamer, Gray Eye? And Black Knife to throw a knife at Smoke Master?"

"She witches everyone to her will, Great Chief." He was not able to maintain eye contact. "She is your assassin, Great Matron." Then, with a sad expression, he looked as honestly into Walks in Moonlight's eyes as he was capable, but his eyes kept darting around the room.

Walks in Moonlight turned to her Council and asked if they had heard enough to make a judgment. Sun on His Face, the oldest member of the Council rose on wobbly legs and addressed his peers, "I have heard enough to know that these men murdered a beloved Dreamer who helped deliver The Son of Morning Star into our midst at a crucial time in the life of this city.

These men must be punished. I say have them taken to the bluff east of the city, dismember them, and let their souls always be lost. Let the animals devour their body parts scattered over the hills. As for the witchcraft charges against the young woman, my opinion is that she is no witch. But her pretty face is beguiling, and I could be mistaken." Many heads nodded in agreement.

"Thank you for your words, Sun on His Face. Does anyone have anything to add?" Walks in Moonlight asked. No one spoke. "Far Gazer, the Sun Clan Council of Elders has questioned the witnesses and the accused in the death of a Great Dreamer. In the questioning, this woman, Bright Moon, or Cass, depending on who is speaking, has been accused of using witchcraft to subdue her enemies, who seem to be many. You may ask further questions or rule as you see fit as Great Sun."

Far Gazer sat for many heartbeats with his chin resting on his fingertips. Finally, he spoke with authority, "It is clear one of the accused has murdered our Great Dreamer, but all four were complicit in the act. As punishment, they will be held prisoner until we know if Smoke Master will live. If he dies, the punishment will be greater. Thank you for your wisdom in this matter Sun on

His Face." He nodded toward Sun on His Face with respect.

"As for the witchcraft charges, they will be considered as a desperate attempt by these criminals to deflect the blame from themselves. This woman is no witch, nor has she used witchcraft. Her use of costumes to mislead her enemy was a brilliant strategy that worked to her advantage. I commend her on her cunning and hope that I never have to face her as an enemy in battle."

Yellow Hair, Bright Moon, and Traveler all breathed a sigh of relief.

*Far Gazer has indeed changed his demeanor since becoming a father!* Traveler thought to himself.

# CHAPTER 17
# SMOKE MASTER WEAKENS

When the temple was cleared, Far Gazer went to the Sun Clan lodge on its high mound east of the Sun Temple Mound where Smoke Master was lying in bed. He was in a weakened state, but coherent. "What is your condition, brother?" Far Gazer stood beside his brother's bed but showed no emotion.

"Brother, my body grows weak. The wound has been invaded by demons, and soon I will walk the Path to the Ancestors. The healers are unable to quiet the demons coursing through my body."

"Why were you with those villains? Did they really surprise you? Or had you arranged to meet them at The Dreamer's lodge?" Far Gazer looked into Smoke Master's bloodshot eyes for honesty.

"Brother, I know I will not live to see many

more sunrises. It is time I confess. It was I who invented the Dreamer's vision that caused you to send the trader looking for a messenger from the sky gods who did not exist. I expected Traveler to return empty-handed, causing you great embarrassment and shame. I had planned for our mother and her Council to place me as Great Sun after stripping you of that title. I wanted ultimate power." His voice was showing how much pain he was in.

"Little brother, why do you think I accepted Traveler and Yellow Hair into the Sun Temple? Have you thought about the work needed to consolidate our power and build this city? Do you think we can get planters, loggers, woodworkers, craftsmen, potters, hunters, gatherers, and the like to do all that needs done just by telling them to do it? Just because they like to work like pack dogs. If you do, you are more foolish than I thought. These people need a reason to do what we ask of them.

"That reason is that WE are related to the gods. It matters little to us if we are or are not, as long as *they* believe it. The way we get them to believe it is to produce a miracle now and then. You see, it makes no difference to us if Yellow Hair is a lost survivor of a storm-tossed sea, or a bloodthirsty raider from some far-off land. If the masses we are trying to control *think* he is a messenger from the sky gods, then that is what he is. If they believe having him there in the Sun Temple will cause the rain to fall and the crops to grow, the woodland and grassland animals to be plentiful, then they will do as we ask of them. But if they think, for a minute, that we are lying to them, that we are mere men, no different than them, everything we have worked for will fall apart.

"So, even though you concocted this great plot of yours to overthrow me, it has worked out to the benefit of our family. And you will continue to play your part as my humble second. Yellow Hair will appear at the Harvest Celebration as a messenger touched by the sky gods. With his yellow hair, who will argue that he is not? And the people will continue to build our city, just as we have planned. My son will preside over the greatest building projects the world has ever seen. You will teach him how to plan and build earthen mounds for temples, clans, death houses, and burials of our important people. I will teach him how to be a god. Do you have any questions? By the way, you will have a guard escort from now on, even outside your sleeping chamber. I do not want anything to happen to my second, after all. I will also have an escort at all times—just to make sure there are no more assassination attempts."

"Brother, have you not listened to me? I am

dying. I will not be here to help you do anything. I do hope that all you are dreaming of comes to pass. I will not be here to interfere. You were always a better visionary than me. You do not need my opinion. You have never asked for it before. Why now? I am merely a decoration attesting to your greatness." His voice trailed off as he closed his eyes, wincing in pain.

"Brother, does the second arrow in a quiver ask why he was not chosen to skewer the deer's heart? No, it simply waits its turn and performs just like the first one did—it is just as important. I expect no less from you. I know how important the Dreamer was to both of us, so let us find a way to honor him as a Great Dreamer. Our people will need something to take their minds off the brutal execution of the would-be assassins." Far Gazer talked as if Smoke Master were wide awake.

"Yes, he will be missed. I wish I could be in his company tonight." Smoke Master barely managed a whisper.

"Rising Moon is no longer a comfort in your sleeping skins?" Far Gazer asked innocently.

"Brother, she has lost all interest in comforting a husband. A child occupies her sleeping skins. And I find no comfort in the arms of a concubine. The Dreamer and I understood one another." Smoke Master's voice had a sadness in it beyond the pain. The earlier fire and anger were gone. After several heartbeats, he continued, "The Dreamer has many tens of tens of shell beads and gorgets in his shop. He worked tirelessly with his hands. He was a true artist."

Far Gazer fingered a Birdman gorget hanging on a cord around his neck. "Yes, I know, he had many talents, and his two spirit powers were beyond any I have known. I never knew his talents until after his wife died." Far Gazer's expression was glum. "We should bury him with great honor. We owe him that. It can be justified by the dream that brought Yellow Hair here as a messenger from the sky gods the same night my son was born. We need to play that up to make it look like our friend, the Dreamer, was bigger than life—that he really did communicate with Eagle Man."

"But what of those who say they have heard of some of the foreigners who look like Yellow Hair? Will they not call this whole *Son of Morning Star* thing a hoax? What if the nonbelievers convince the crowds that we have lied to them? I think having this Yellow Hair around so people learn that he is really just a man could be dangerous." Smoke Master muttered painfully, sweat beading on his forehead.

"Perhaps you are right, brother. Maybe our guest should disappear after the Harvest Celebration. Let me ponder this. In the meantime, let us not talk to anyone about this. The trader could be a problem too, he knows us too well and Yellow Hair better than anyone else. And the woman, she must go as well. Perhaps Sun Seer has some ideas." Far Gazer spoke as he thought.

"Or our mother, she *is* the Head Matron of Sun Clan." Smoke Master could feel his strength draining as he spoke.

## CHAPTER 18
# CHANGES

T raveler, Yellow Hair, and Bright Moon left the Sun Temple and made their way toward the plaza when a runner stopped them and told Traveler that Walks in Moonlight wanted to speak to them.

After formal pleasantries were exchanged the Head Matron started, "Your stories are incredible, quite difficult to believe, but seemingly backed by the facts. I still find it hard to believe this woman is capable of the deeds she has supposedly accomplished. And her sister went through all the same things, even killed men, but now has settled into ordinary domestic life? Hard to believe, I must say. Is there more that my ears have not heard?" She directed the questions to Traveler so he could translate.

Traveler spoke briefly with Yellow Hair and Bright Moon. "Head Matron, the stories have been related to you in detail with no omissions. Both these young people have been through horrific trials and have emerged as strong warriors. Surprisingly, neither harbor hate in their hearts. They both hope that their trials are behind them, and they just wish to lead ordinary lives going forward."

"Ah, the foolish young at heart!" Walks in Moonlight snickered. "Trials do not end for anyone. And after what they have been through, especially for them. Can they not see that every trial prepares a person for the next one? These two, though they bleed like everyone else and could die like everyone else, have been chosen for more than they have experienced so far. Only the gods know what is in their future, but I am confident there are more trials to come for these two.

"I think it will be better that they move into the Sun Clan lodge where they will be my guests at least until the harvest ceremonies are completed. We will figure something else out then. Traveler, you will move in with them to translate until they have mastered our tongue. Go now and gather your things. Raven Wing will escort you and show you to your places. This is all I have to say."

"As you wish, Great Matron." Traveler did not

look at Yellow Hair or Bright Moon. They under-stood enough to know that their lives were changing again.

Once outside the lodge as they made their way across the plaza, Traveler told them what Walks in Moonlight had said.

"I do not think this is a good arrangement. Do you think there is any way we can refuse?" Bright Moon asked so that Raven Wing would not understand.

"Not a chance. The Head Matron has spoken. I think she fears others might wish you harm and wants to protect you—at least for now."

"I do not like it," Yellow Hair chimed in. "We will still be prisoners. Maybe we should think about going back to Monongahela Village."

"No!" Bright Moon snapped. "My life there has ended. I cannot go back." She did not know where the words came from because she was thinking it would be nice to see Bright Star.

Traveler and Yellow Hair looked at her with mouths gaping open. "Where did that come from?" Yellow Hair was surprised by his wife's outburst.

"I do not know! That is not what I was think-ing, but somehow, I know it is the truth. I cannot go back, no more than you can go back to your Norway. We should go farther west, I think."

Again, she blurted it out, saying what was not on her mind.

"Right now, we cannot go anywhere except to the Sun Clan lodge. Our escort will see to that." Traveler knew Raven Wing would follow orders.

"Yes, let us get there so we can plan our escape." Bright Moon had that old, determined look in her eye.

Traveler looked at Yellow Hair. "Your wife is a remarkable woman."

"I know!"

When they got back to the Sun Clan lodge late in the afternoon, only servants were present. They directed the guests to a newly partitioned section of the lodge where lounging mats of woven cattail leaves were laid out on the floor and two sleeping platforms were newly built with a hanging deer skin partition between them. Both would accommodate two people.

# CHAPTER 19
# A FUNERAL

S un Seer, High Priest of the Sun Clan entered the main room of the Sun Temple to find Walks in Moonlight and Far Gazer seated on the dais in a quiet discussion. "Greetings Great Sun, I hope this day finds you feeling well. The late summer weather has been perfect for the ripening corn. It looks as if it will be another big harvest. Your leadership is being rewarded by the gods."

"Greetings to you, High Priest. On behalf of myself and the Head Matron, we welcome you. I hope the summons did not interrupt anything requiring your presence. We have some important things to talk about."

"I am always at your service, Great Sun." The high priest bowed to his master.

"I trust the Shell Clan priests are nearly finished preparing the Dreamer's body for burial. We wish to honor the man with a great funeral to celebrate his fantastic dream that foretold the birth of my son, who will one day be the reincarnation of The Morning Star in this world and preside over the city. We were just discussing how we should honor the deceased Dreamer. Let us hear what your suggestions are."

"Great Sun, I am but a servant to you and the other gods who control our lives. I do your bidding. Shall we start by you giving me your ideas and together we can work out how to incorporate them into a great ceremony? Before we start on that, what is Smoke Master's condition?" Sun Seer demonstrated his loyalty with his subservient behavior.

"He fears he is dying, but we have our greatest healers working tirelessly to return him to health. I have confidence he will recover." Only Far Gazer felt Smoke Master would survive the evil that had entered his body.

"The idea is to honor the deceased while establishing the power and compassion of the Sun Clan. To demonstrate how we grieve for the Shell Clan's loss, and yet how the Dreamer's epic dream consolidated the sky gods' faith in the Sun Clan's ability to build this great city. That the Dreamer's life was given so all of Cahokia would prosper." Walks in Moonlight's calm words to the priest showed no emotion.

"And we should incorporate the Dreamer's artwork to show Eagle Man how worthy he was—how hard the Dreamer worked to praise Eagle Man."

A ten-and-six-summers-old young man wearing a plain white shirt and breechclout with a knee length apron tentatively walked to the center in front of the dais and nervously blurted out, "Smoke Master is crying out for Far Gazer and Walks in Moonlight to come to his chamber. He looks as if death is upon him."

Walks in Moonlight entered Smoke Master's chamber and stood next to his bed. The stench of rotting flesh assaulted her nostrils. Without flinching, she took up his hand. It felt as if it were on fire. "How can I help you, my son?"

"I...wanted...to...say...farewell...m...mother." Smoke Master gasped between painful cramps.

"You cannot die. Will yourself to fight this demon that has invaded your body and souls." She remained stoic, knowing there was nothing she, or anyone could do to save him.

Far Gazer noted the others standing around

the chamber. Smoke Master's wife, their ten-summers-old son, his house servant holding her five-summers-old child, his wife's twin sister and her husband, and the healer, Cedar Smoke. Cedar Smoke was chanting to himself and shaking a small turtle-shell rattle in one hand and a falcon wing in the other. Despite the people in the chamber, each wearing various scented oils, and the healer's cedar incense burning in a small ceramic pot in a corner, the odor from Smoke Master's wound dominated the room.

Smoke Master feebly asked Far Gazer to come to his bed. He weakly held his hand up for Far Gazer to take. "It is time to say goodbye, brother. May your wisdom guide our people wisely. I will watch over you from the next world..." His grip failed and sleep overcame him. Far Gazer patted him gently on the head, turned and walked away. Smoke Master never regained consciousness. Within two hands of time, he took his final breath.

———

"OUR FUNERAL PLANS have become more complex." Walks in Moonlight spoke to Far Gazer the evening Smoke Master died.

"Yes. No funeral has been more important since my father's." Far Gazer gazed into the fire pit.

"The funeral will take place the first morning of the Harvest Celebration, and the burial will be next to the burial site of my late husband and near the old Solstice post close by where the old charnel house was located. A mound aligning with the Solstice sunrise will be built up over the old and new graves so that it is in full view of the sky gods." Walks in Moonlight stated in a way that made it clear there would be no discussion on the subject.

"This funeral should be a spectacle the people will always remember. A tribute to the sky gods, one that shows our family's closeness to them. A pageant." Far Gazer's words and demeanor demonstrated his eyes were on the future with no remorse for his brother's death.

"Smoke Master's entire line should be included so that no one can ever dispute your authority."

"What are you saying, Mother?" The Great Sun's eyes were wide open now and looking into hers.

"His wife, his surviving son, her sister and husband, his personal servants and child. Everyone with close ties to him." Walks in Moonlight showed no more emotion than Far Gazer.

"We will put the Dreamer in that grave as well, and his young wife who died two winters past. She rests in the Shell Clan charnel house."

"Why would we include the Dreamer in a Sun Clan burial?"

"Because they were lovers. My brother inspired the dream that brought Yellow Hair here. We can tie it all together. The Dream, Yellow Hair's arrival to signify the incarnation of The Morning Star, the assassins of the Underworld trying to disrupt the flow of divine power into the Sun Clan, our triumph over their treachery through the sacrifice of our own blood. It is perfect. The people will do anything we ask of them from this point forward." Far Gazer had a gleam in his eye now.

"What about Yellow Hair and this woman of his? She scares me. No woman should be as strong as she is." Walks in Moonlight had genuine concern in her voice.

"Give me some time to come up with a plan for their demise." Far Gazer smiled. "Perhaps the sky gods will demand more sacrifices at the next Harvest Celebration?" She smiled back uneasily.

———

AT SUNRISE on the first day of the Harvest Celebration, which coincided with the fall equinox, a loud pot drum sounded a single beat at the location of the old Solstice post south of the new grand plaza that echoed throughout the city and beyond.

The sun rose into a clear sky that lit up the trees in the early stages of turning to their fall colors. Hackberries and cottonwoods were already fading from summer green to hints of their autumn yellows. A few oaks on the hillsides were beginning the transition to golden brown, and the sumacs and choke cherries were already a brilliant scarlet color. Cornstalks stripped of their full ears stood drying in the fields as yellowed husks of their former selves. Still green bean vines clung to the bare stalks. Orange pumpkins, green and yellow squash lay randomly in the rows between the Corn stalks. The grasslands gave off a golden hue of mixed shades of yellows, purples, oranges, and greens.

A second drum sounded from the north end of the plaza where two-tens-of-tens of drummers lined up at the base of The Great Sun Mound under construction. All those drums began a somber beat that could be heard echoing up and down the valley of the Grandfather River. Five-tens of flute players joined them as a procession from the base of the existing Sun Mound started across the plaza, then turning toward the south.

Leading the procession was the Sun Clan head priest, Sun Seer. He wore a one-piece, white doeskin gown with long, oversized sleeves made with a big sunburst of white columellate beads on the chest. Following him was The Great Sun, Far Gazer with his mother, Head Matron of the Sun Clan, Walks in Moonlight. She wore a long sleeve, deep maroon colored, finely woven fabric dress decorated with shell, quill, and bead chevrons and sunburst designs on the sleeves, shoulders and just above the short-fringed hem below her knees. Tall black moccasins with fawn hoof rattles on the top of each foot adorned her feet. Her gray hair was braided and curled around her head and held in place with copper hair pins decorated with sunbursts, eagles, falcons, hawks, and ravens. Blue eye paint surrounded her eyes, accented by the white forked-eye design of the sky gods.

Far Gazer wore a dark-blue colored buckskin shirt with fringe running down the sleeves and bottom hem just below his waist sash. The shirt was decorated with a yellow sunburst painted on the chest and quill thunderbirds depicted on the shoulders. His skirt was a brilliant, white-colored buckskin with fringe running down the front flap that came to a point between his knees. His moccasins were dark blue with thunderbirds made from porcupine quills on the tops of each foot. His gray-sprinkled black hair was in a single braid twisted on top of his head and held in place by a dark-blue doeskin turban secured with a copper pin depicting a sunburst. Copper ear spools decorated with images of the long-nosed god were embedded in his earlobes. From a copper and buckskin braided thong around his neck hung a gorget made of shell with Eagle Man soaring in a blue sky. A single eagle feather hung from the top of his turban down over the back of his neck. Above his beaded forelock, a blue spirit box was held in place by two copper pins with the Hero Twins carved on flat heads. A black sash around his waist was pinned with a copper falcon pin and hung down near his left knee.

Following Far Gazer and Walks in Moonlight was Far Gazer's young wife, Morning Light carrying the newborn, Star. Beside Morning Light was Yellow Hair. Much to Yellow Hair's dismay, somewhere in the massive crowd of spectators were Bright Moon and Traveler. Morning Light's attire identified her as Star Clan, and Yellow Hair was given the plain dark brown fabric tunic and leggings of a midlevel Sun Clan priest. He wore his hair in a single braid down his back and tied off with a black buckskin thong. Large blue ovals surrounded his eyes and the forked symbol of the sky gods, painted white, radiated across his temples.

Behind them were members of the seven additional clans that made up the rulers of Cahokia. Each group included the clan head matron, civil chief (usually the husband, son, or brother of the Head Matron), and priest. They were each dressed symbolizing their clan. Behind them were young men bearing ten litters carrying bodies for burial. Following the litters were the clan elders of the hunters, loggers, potters, and other craftsmen. Behind them were the head matrons and civil chiefs of each of the planter clans. Tens of tens of tens of spectators of all the clans and visitors lined the route from the base of the Sun Mound to the burial site south of the plaza. Visitors from all directions were in town for the Harvest Celebration. Visiting dignitaries fell in behind the planter clans.

North and east of the place where the big Solstice Pole once stood was a low mound about four man-heights across and half a man-height tall. The middle section of the mound was removed, and a triangular pit was dug about knee deep, three man-lengths on a side with the point toward the northwest. The pit was layered with white clay. A section of white clay a little longer and wider than a man was covered with black clay. On the black clay were many seashell beads laid out in the shape of a standing eagle. This bead bed was roughly the size of a man.

When the litter procession arrived, the drums and flutes stopped. The litters were laid on the ground outside the excavated pit. Sun Seer stepped up onto a small wooden platform built to raise him above the crowd of people who had gathered. The platform was set just to the east of the location of the place where the large Solstice Pole had been removed.

The clan elders were on the east side of Sun Seer, and the masses of spectators were arranged west and northwest of the burial pit. Sun Seer removed the fringed white buckskin bag he had carried over his shoulder. From it he took a ceremonial pipe made of red stone and carved to resemble Eagle Man. An attendant boy came up and handed him a pouch with sacred tobacco in it. The boy then retrieved a lit brand from a small fire pit east of the platform while the priest filled the bowl. Once lit, the priest puffed and chanted toward the sun, then toward the burial pit floor. Next, he chanted and puffed in each of the four sacred directions. Finally, he puffed toward the northeast where the sun rose in the sky on the morning of the Summer Solstice, and once toward the northwest where the sun set on that day. He then knocked the dottle out of the pipe and handed it to the boy, who held it until the bowl cooled, after which he put it back in the white bag.

At the priest's instruction, the various remains were placed in the grave. First came the wife of the brother of Far Gazer. She was placed on the bed of shell beads and a beaded blanket was spread over her legs and up to her waist. Then Far Gazer's brother was placed directly over her. The two of them were dressed in skirts made of sequentially arranged shell beads and wore several beads for decorations around their necks and laid on their chests. Far Gazer's brother wore a fine shell brooch. More beads were poured over his body while Far Gazer stood on the raised platform and eulogized his brother.

Next, their ten-summers-old son was laid next to the bed of beads on the southwest side. On the other side of Far Gazer's brother was placed the remains of his other brother and wife who had been deceased for several sun cycles. Next to his brother and off the bead bed were the murdered Dreamer along with the bundled remains of his wife who had been dead for over two sun cycles. Just off the eagle's head of beads and placed perpendicular to the other bodies were those of Far Gazer's brother's two men and two women attendants. Along with one of the couples was their five-summers-old son.

Sun Seer told the crowd about each body, citing which had been murdered, which had died of natural causes, and which had volunteered to escort The Great Sun's second to the afterlife among their ancestors in the Sky World. The priest stepped down from the platform as Far Gazer continued his performance.

Far Gazer spent some time telling of the importance of the Dreamer and his dream that brought Yellow Hair to Cahokia, foretelling the future re-quickening of Star into Morning Star. How that event will bring a new light to the world, and Cahokia will be the center of the greatest achievements of man in the world. He tied all the recent events together and claimed how this day would long be remembered.

Then, he added that this was just the beginning and that The Great Sun Mound would place The Great Sun above the trees so that the Sky World gods could communicate directly with him. The greatness of Cahokia would never diminish. The mound and palace would be completed for the re-quickening of The Morning Star, and he would rule from a great palace atop the great mound.

A drum sounded, signaling the ceremony had ended, and people began to move back toward the plaza. Raven Wing's warriors surrounded and escorted the ruling clan elders and priests back to the north while the lesser clans were permitted to disperse on their own. Far Gazer informed Yellow

Hair that he would be expected to take a place on the Sun Clan chunkey team in the games later in the day.

Yellow Hair's mind was on finding Bright Moon and Traveler to make sure they were safe in the huge crowd.

# CHAPTER 20

# A PROBLEM IS
# RECOGNIZED

Far Gazer gave Yellow Hair permission to go find his wife, provided he was on the plaza chunkey court by midafternoon dressed in the Sun Clan chunkey player costume, which would be delivered to his chamber. A palace guard accompanied Yellow Hair to ensure The Great Sun's orders were followed.

After Yellow Hair changed into his plain hunting shirt, plain breechclout, and leggings, he set out to find Bright Moon and Traveler. They had planned to meet at the trader booths midmorning, but it was already late morning.

———

FAR GAZER, Walks in Moonlight, and Sun Seer met in the Sun Clan Temple after Yellow Hair left. "What do you think we should do with him?" Far Gazer asked his guests.

"He seems to have no ill intent as far as I can tell. But just having him in Cahokia raises many questions about who he really is. My informants tell me that everyone wants to look upon him, to touch his yellow hair, and look into his sky-blue eyes. The novelty is showing no sign of diminishing. And now he is out among them. I hope it does not lead to some sort of trouble.

"And that woman of his—her reputation as a mankiller has spread far and wide. Many young warriors want to conquer her—in more ways than one. I might add, she *is* quite attractive, although she dresses too plain for an important man's wife. I fear only trouble can come from them being in the city." Walks in Moonlight moved her gaze to each of the others present.

"Yes, and while he does not disclaim or ridicule our religious beliefs, he clings to his one god philosophy like it cannot be changed. His talk around campfires could be dangerous to our way of life." Sun Seer demonstrated his concern with his uncertain voice and darting eyes.

"We are agreed that he cannot stay in Cahokia then. The question is, how do we rid ourselves of this problem? If we exile him and the woman, our people may see it as us repulsing a messenger from the Sky World. That could make them lose faith in us. And anywhere he goes, he could stir up trouble for us.

"We could make a spectacle of sacrificing them, telling the masses that was the intent of Eagle Man from the start. Once the message about Morning Star was delivered, the mortal body of the man was to be given to the Underworld gods while his life soul was to return to the Sky World." Far Gazer offered his suggestion without emotion.

"Son, these people saved your life ten-and-five nights past. I think you owe them more than a slit throat. I have talked to them and found them honorable people, even though I will be happier once they leave. It could truly offend the gods to sacrifice them. The man and woman man may yet have a role to play in building this city. I say we should keep them alive as our guests. We should keep an eye on them to make sure they have no plans to betray us. In time, some sign will be given as to what we should do with them."

"Priest?" Far Gazer looked to Sun Seer.

"Too bad there is no place to send them, like as emissaries or something. It would not be uncommon for some dreadful accident to befall such travelers." Sun Seer left the idea out there.

"We could send them to the mud-brick temple builders in the mesa country to learn their ways of sun worship. I understand that those people are fighting among themselves. It could be a dangerous place." Walks in Moonlight studied the other faces for reaction.

"Perhaps they could go among the buffalo hunters in the great grasslands. We could use more tribute from those people, and their nomadic life is very tenuous."

"There are many possibilities. Perhaps we can settle on a course of action once the Harvest Celebration is over. Let us think on it. Mother, do keep in touch with your informants. We need to stay in the know concerning the mood of the people. We will meet like this again when all the visitors have left town. Perhaps Yellow Hair will get into some misunderstanding during this celebration and meet with an untimely end." Far Gazer ended their discussion, stood, and walked out of the Sun Clan Temple.

# CHAPTER 21

# POMP AND CEREMONY

Yellow Hair did not have to worry that it would take long to find Bright Moon. She was right at the base of the Sun Clan Mound talking to Raven Wing and waiting for Yellow Hair to finish his *messenger from the sky gods* duties. Yellow Hair's guard gave Raven Wing a salute. They bid farewell to Raven Wing and moved through the crowds to Traveler's trading booth, closely followed by the guard escort. "Where did he come from?" Bright Moon jerked her thumb toward the guard behind them. She was using the Monongahela tongue so the guard would not know what she asked.

"Courtesy of The Great Sun. The man does not want his *Sky Messenger* running into any trouble on this solemn day. And I am to be ready to play chunkey this afternoon. They even set a fine dress out for you to wear. I am not sure what to think. They bring us into their circle, but they do not trust us. For me, the feeling is mutual. I wish I knew what they wanted from us and what they are planning if we cannot deliver."

After the funeral pageant was over, Traveler had done a brisk business trading off many of the goods Painted Turtle and Corn Stalk had furnished him. The piebald deer hide that Otter had donated was a most sought-after prize.

Traveler told them that everyone was asking about Yellow Hair. It seems his presence was causing quite a stir. And countless young wannabe warriors were asking about the mankiller woman from the Spirit River lands.

Yellow Hair told them he could not stay long. He had to get ready to compete in the chunkey games for the Sun Clan. Bright Moon said she wanted to play but learned unequivocally that women were not allowed in the men's games.

Traveler warned Yellow Hair, "Play well enough to make sure the Sun Clan wins but try not to draw much attention to yourself. The Great Sun gets jealous when someone besides him gets much adoration."

"I do not even know what rules they play here.

I will probably make a fool of myself." Yellow Hair shook his head.

"That will never happen!" Bright Moon swooned.

When the sun passed its peak in the cloudless sky, Yellow Hair and Bright Moon worked back through the crowd to the Sun Clan mound and lodge, their escort still on their heels. Countless people touched Yellow Hair's head as they walked toward the Sun Clan mound.

Although she could not play, Bright Moon would be expected, as a guest of the Sun Clan, to wear a fine dress and cheer from the sidelines as her husband competed against the best chunkey players in the world.

In their chamber, they found a player's costume for Yellow Hair to put on and an elegant dress with accessories for Bright Moon to wear to the games. As soon as they entered, a male attendant came to Yellow Hair and told him he first must get to the sweat lodge for a session, then apply his body paint before putting on the special breechclout, skirt, moccasins, and headdress. A female attendant came to Bright Moon and told her she would escort her to the creek to bathe, then help her get dressed and ready for the big event.

Bright Moon's dress was a light, tan-colored

doeskin with long sleeves and fringes down the sleeves and bottom with a mid-calf hem. A bright yellow sunburst decorated the chest with red, white, blue, and yellow bead chevrons on the shoulders. A red fabric belt tied around the waist with a copper eagle pin securing the knot. The ends of the sash fell to mid-thigh. New buckskin moccasins came to the top of her calves and turned over with a fringed hem. The four-sacred-colored beaded spirals adorned the top of the feet. Where these clothes came from or who made them was a mystery to Bright Moon, but they fit her perfectly.

Next, her attendant oiled and scented her hair with bear grease and linden flowers. Her hair was still not long enough to braid, so a buckskin head band held her hair tightly to her head, down behind her ears and almost to her collar. A braid of another woman's hair was attached to the back of the headband and hung down nearly to her waist. Red-tailed hawk tail feathers were entwined in the stranger's hair. Wearing another woman's hair caused Bright Moon some uneasiness, but the attendant assured her it was a normal thing—many women donated their hair for such occasions.

*Kind of like those attendants donated their lives to be buried with The Great Sun's brother, I suppose. I wonder if I am wearing a dead woman's hair.*

Armbands of woven cloth in the four sacred colors were tied to her upper arms. When the attendant was satisfied with Bright Moon's appearance, she escorted her into the big room in the front of the Sun Clan lodge.

Yellow Hair was covered with bear grease mixed with mint and white ash to make his skin look almost white. A large yellow sunburst was painted on his chest. A red and black depiction of Eagle Man was painted on his back. A large eagle feather was painted on each arm and an eagle leg with talons spread down each leg. He was given a new red breechclout and skirt with black fringe hanging near his knees in a triangle. His hair was plaited into a single braid and wrapped around the top of his head where it was held in place with four bone pins with eagle heads carved into the ends. Next a woven human hair headdress was placed on top of his head and held in place with more bone eagle headed pins. The woven hair was dyed the color of a golden eagle's head and shaped to match. A wooden beak painted yellow made him look like a bigger-than-life eagle head adorned his skull. He hoped he would be given a chance to practice with this awkward headpiece attached to his head.

After he was fully dressed and painted, the attendant escorted him behind the Sun Clan lodge where the other players were standing in a loose group talking. Each was dressed depicting a different sky god. One was Falcon, another was Thunderbird, another was Raven, and another was Hawk. Only Hawk did not wear the ungainly head-dress. His was merely a smallish hood with an actual red-tailed hawk's head at the top of the forehead. He would be the chunkey roller. All the players, including Yellow Hair, wore a beaded fore-lock down the center of their foreheads. Yellow Hair's was made by braiding a section of his hair and doubling it back so that it would not be in his eyes. Each of the players' forelock hair was kept together by threading it through beads of the four sacred colors.

Four other women around Bright Moon's age and dressed similarly were talking quietly in a group. The attendant brought her to that group and introduced her. They were the wives or concu-bines of the other men on the Sun Clan chunkey team. The first question she was asked was if Yellow Hair had ever played chunkey before. She assured them that he had, and he was skilled, but not as good as her. They gave her a hearty laugh. She got the feeling they thought it was a joke.

One woman, whose bulging belly said she was with child asked, "What is it like being the wife of a sky god messenger?"

That caught Bright Moon off guard, and she thought about answering that he was no messenger from the gods but being with him made her feel like a goddess. She reconsidered and just answered the best she could that he acted like an ordinary man. She could understand the Cahokia tongue alright now, but still had some difficulty speaking it.

Another of the women chided her, "Oh come now, I am sure his manhood makes you soar through the clouds!"

The others laughed.

Bright Moon just blushed and smiled. *What can I say? That is true!* She kept that thought to herself. Small talk ensued about how exciting life in Cahokia was at the time. All the new people coming to the town, the new building projects, the great ceremonies, and dances. It was all as Far Gazer, and his family had foreseen it would be.

In time, Walks in Moonlight joined them, and attendants served more tea before they left for the chunkey court. A squad of Raven Wing's warriors escorted the Sun Clan elders and the player's wives to their designated place beside the central chunkey court in the middle of the great plaza.

Once all the important spectators were in place behind him, Far Gazer announced the opening of the chunkey games that would last until a final victor was named. He gave the usual speech about how good all the teams were and that The Great Sun wishes them all the best of luck and may the best team win. Everyone knew that the Sun Clan would not be denied the most wins.

By draw, the first two teams to compete were the Sun Clan and the Star Clan. Next would come the Moon Clan against the Earth Clan. The third match would be Water against Fire. The fourth match would feature the Wind Clan against the Cloud Clan.

## CHAPTER 22
# CHUNKEY

The chunkey court was laid out in a rectangle centered next to the great cedar post in the middle of the great plaza, its long side running east and west. Near the east end of the court was a line marked with ash and running north and south. The players would start at that line. Ten paces to the west was another ash line. The throwers would release their chunkey sticks and stop before they reached that line. Ten paces to the west of that line was another. The roller would stop at that line while he released the stone, rolling it toward the west.

At a signal, the roller from each team would advance past the first line. As soon as he crossed that line, the throwers could advance. The roller would release the stone just before the throwers released their sticks. From the way the roller set the stone rolling, the throwers needed to predict where the stone would go and try to land their sticks close to where the stone stopped. The distances to the stone would be tallied.

For tiebreakers, rings on the sticks would be used to determine the lowest number of rings to the point of the stick. As such, if a player from each team landed their stick within a hand of the stone and one landed so that the front of the stone was closest to the third ring and the player from the other team was four rings, the one with the three rings would be given the lowest distance.

The team with the lowest total distance would win a point. The first team to two-tens of points would win and move on to the next round, winning teams playing winning teams until one team was left. Side bets were placed by the spectators on each team and on individual players. While great glory was placed on the winning team and best individuals, great shame was heaped on the losers.

Yellow Hair and the others stepped out onto the newly brushed court. It was as smooth as a baby's skin. Not a flaw could be seen as Yellow Hair studied the surface trying to determine how the chunkey stone might roll.

While he was doing that, he was also admiring

the chunkey stick he had been handed. From the ground, it came up to about the bottom of his ribs. It was no more than a knuckle in diameter and tapered to a point on both ends, which had been fire hardened. It was painted yellow, to match the eagle beak on his head, with black marks about a half of a hand-width apart from end to end. Holding it in the middle, he found it perfectly balanced and figured it would go wherever he willed it to. The feel of it made him smile.

He looked at the crowd of ruling clans and saw Bright Moon with the Sun Clan group. His eyes fixed on her radiance as they exchanged smiles.

An elder announced that the players advance to the first line. The Sun Clan team assembled on a line that marked the starting position. The Star Clan players lined up to their left and gave their most evil expressions to the Sun Clan players. The roller stood in the middle of each team and held the stone in his right hand in front of him. He was the oldest player on each team and advised his fellow players how he would release the stone so they could better predict its course.

On a signal, the rollers advanced, and when they crossed the thrower line, the throwers advanced drawing their sticks back into a throwing position. Yellow Hair concentrated on keeping his head up so that the headdress would not make him lose balance. He watched the roller dip his shoulder and release the stone smoothly so that it rolled straight up the court. Calculating the stone's speed and distance, he released his stick and stopped before the throwers' line.

To Yellow Hair the world seemed to slow down as he watched the four chunkey sticks arch through the sky. All four seemed to fly above the throngs of spectators in unison toward an unseen target. The sticks reached a high point in their trajectory and started back toward the court. The drum he was hearing turned out to be his own blood pounding in his ears. As the sticks dove back toward the ground, the rolling chunkey stone came into view. It rolled in a true straight line, barely bobbing on the smooth surface of the court, leaving a concave trail in the thin layer of dust on the manicured surface.

The stone slowed and came to a stop as the sticks began to land around it. Falcon's blue stick hit the ground first, the leading point penetrated the brushed clay surface and stuck at a low angle less than half a pace right in front of the stone. Next Thunderbird's red stick landed hard on its side and slid to a stop within a hand on the right side of the stone and the leading edge of the stone at the second line on the stick. Next, Raven's black stick landed on its side on the left side of the stone and slid to a stop at the third white ring. Finally, Yellow Hair watched his own yellow lance plummet to the ground and stick into the court surface a half a pace behind the stone. A cheer rose from the Sun Clan spectators. Four well placed shots, taken all together.

Yellow Hair looked over and saw that the yellow-striped, blue stick of the Star Clan team had landed and slid past the stone more than a pace. The three other sticks were less than a pace from the stone. Everyone was happy except the Star Clan players and supporters. Many of the spectators had bet against the Sun Clan because they had not seen Yellow Hair play chunkey before. His longest distance was still closer than Star Clan's longest, giving the Sun Clan the point. A chorus of cheers reverberated across the plaza and echoed off the trees in the distance.

Designated elders came forth and marked sticks that matched the color of each chunkey stick with an obsidian knife. The end of each of the sticks featured a carved figure matching the character of the thrower's headdress. Another set of sticks with a carving depicting the clan was marked showing the team's total distance. When those sticks were marked, the elders officially announced the Sun Clan the winner of the point. The game continued until the Sun Clan team accumulated two-tens of score sticks. The Star Clan had accumulated ten-and-four points. The Sun Clan advanced.

A group of men dressed in plain tan shirts and leggings entered the court and swept all the marks from the first game away using turkey wings. When they were finished, the court looked as though it had never been used.

The next game was between the Moon Clan and Earth Clan. The Earth Clan won by about the same margin as the Sun Clan had. The third game between the Water and Fire Clans resulted in the Water Clan as winners. In the fourth game between the Wind and Cloud Clans, the Cloud Clan came out victorious.

The Cloud and Sun Clans then played to see who would play in the final game. This time, Raven's stick came to a rest touching the stone at the first ring, Falcon's was less than a hand away at the second ring, Yellow Hair's was a hand away at the fourth ring and Thunderbird's was two hands away at the second ring. In the end, they beat Cloud Clan by two points. The match between Water and Earth Clans resulted in Earth Clan winning by two points. That set up the final match between Sun Clan and Earth Clan.

Many drums, flutes, and dancers entertained the crowds while the chunkey court was being groomed for the final match. When the court was ready, a special drumbeat brought the other drums and dancers to a halt. Everyone moved back to their places while an elder announced the final game of the Harvest Celebration High Chunkey Matches. With much flourish and ceremony, the Sun Clan Priest smoked a ceremonial pipe with the bowl made of red stone carved depicting The Morning Star as a chunkey player. He puffed in the four sacred directions, the sky gods, and the Underworld gods.

Far Gazer came forward and, through a special amplifying horn, explained that the chunkey games were more than games, that they exemplified their great society and symbolized the ties between the Sky World and the earth. He recited how the Hero Twins went into the Underworld and defeated the Underworld players and brought their father back to life.

At last, the game could be played. The sun was approaching the western horizon. Yellow Hair stepped up to the start line with a nervous stomach. He was placed next to the roller for the first time. That would change his throwing angle, and he was trying to calculate by how much when the start signal was given. He advanced and let his stick fly without ever concluding how much his angle should change. He just went on his natural instincts. His stick came down and stuck in the court as the stone rolled to a stop less than a hand from the stick's point. Thunderbird's slid to a stop closer than Yellow Hair's. Falcon's slid up to Thunderbird's and stopped at the first ring. Raven's came to a rest less than a hand's width to the side and the point even with the front of the chunkey stone.

Earth Clan's sticks also clustered around their stone. When all distances were totaled, the Sun Clan won the point by two finger widths—less than one ring. Cheers rang through the plaza and reverberated off the lodges and trees in the distance. The game went on, with the Sun Clan winning by four points.

With great pomp and circumstance, The Great Sun placed a pendant over each Sun Clan player's head. On the pendant was an engraved copper plate that pictured a chunkey player with a stone at his feet and a stick in his right hand. The player wore a mask and was dressed like the Sun Clan players.

Bright Moon hugged each of the other player's wives and shouted above the noise "Yellow Hair can play chunkey!" They each nodded and smiled.

The plaza erupted into an ordered chaos as the sun descended beyond the hills in the west. Several dance circles were formed in different locations around the plaza with a central fire pit and booths serving corn cakes flavored with blueberries and currants, tea of different concoctions, and most popular, black drink.

The high-ranked clans had their own circle and stayed there with their peers. They had bison, elk, pronghorn, and deer meat roasting, stews featuring several meats, fish—mussels, and crayfish, corn and squash cakes, and acorn and nut breads flavored with honey.

Traveler joined Yellow Hair and Bright Moon to interpret, but learned his services were only needed when Yellow Hair or Bright Moon had to give long descriptions of their adventures. The young women marveled at Bright Moon's stories while they backed slightly away from her. None wanted to be too close to a mankiller, though they admired and were somewhat jealous of her prowess. Everyone wanted to get close to Yellow Hair. Many demanded that he speak in his native tongue. They laughed at his Norse words and accent.

Soon enough they were dancing and feeling the effect of the black drink. Yellow Hair was having difficulty keeping his balance with the awkward headdress and Bright Moon grew tired before she expected to. They snuck off to their chamber long before the drums ceased playing shortly before a new day started.

Later that morning, long after the sun had risen, Bright Moon awoke to a queasy stomach and a headache. She vowed to take it easy on the black drink from that day onward. The day brought many speeches, mostly about the greatness of Cahokia, and now with Yellow Hair's message, the city and its leaders would become even more powerful. The divinity of the Sun Clan had been proven and future events would be even more significant. Word would spread along the great rivers that Cahokia will be the center of power in the future and unto eternity, linked forever with the sky gods.

A Green Corn Ceremony was carried out featuring long-winded speeches by clan priests, feasts with the newly harvested corn as the center attraction, drum and flute music, and many hands of time of dancing. Again, Bright Moon grew tired well before the music and dancing ended near dawn.

The rest of the Harvest Celebration played out with the lower-ranked clans holding their chunkey games. The number of spectators diminished, and the court was not as well groomed. The quality of the stones, sticks, and costumes diminished, but the importance of the games to the players did not.

When the last game was played, Bright Moon asked her sisterhood of Sun Clan player's wives, "When do we get to play?" Their reply was laughter.

"It is a man's game, silly," one finally answered when she noticed that Bright Moon was serious.

"But I thought everyone in Cahokia played." Bright Moon bristled.

"Women only play when they are children. No one teaches us the finer skills after our first moon. There is no chance for us to learn to get better." The wife of the player representing Raven shrugged her shoulders and took a long draught of black drink.

"I know how. I learned in Squirrel Tail Village up on the Spirit River. I could teach you if we could get stones and sticks." Bright Moon tried to gain support.

"They will not let us. Forget it." Primrose, escort of Falcon Man, also took a big swallow of black drink.

"I will talk to Walks in Moonlight, surely the Head Matron could help us get some women's games going," Bright Moon persisted but got no support.

"Good luck." Primrose walked away from her.

# CHAPTER 23
# THUNDER THROAT VISITS

I n the following days, Bright Moon began to wake up with that queasy feeling in her stomach. Her appetite vanished in the morning, but it was back with a vengeance in the afternoon. She found herself hoarding corn cakes to eat at night when she woke up hungry. She blamed her odd feelings on the craziness surrounding the Harvest Celebration, the exotic foods, and different drinks. The harvest moon was ending, and the hunter's moon would soon be upon them. Each night she wondered why Far Gazer or Walks in Moonlight had not told them they had to move out of the Sun Clan lodge.

*Cass slowly became aware from out of a foggy darkness. Her head felt like a mortar that had a log pestle pounding corn in it all night. Her teeth were broken, jagged stumps along her gum lines. She could not move her lower jaw, and it felt misshapen, broken. The taste of old vomit clung to her tongue. She was unable to move her arms or legs. She was staked out, spread eagle on a moist forest floor, and completely naked. Tens of tens of mosquitoes were voraciously sucking blood from every part of her body. Slowly she realized her lower abdomen was cramping, much worse than normal moon cramps.*

*Suddenly, from out of nowhere, Thunder Throat came into her view. He also was completely naked. He was painted head to toe with narrow, alternating, vertical red and black stripes. The area around his eyes was painted black like a raccoon. The whites of his eyes were yellow and bloodshot, the pupils were bottomless black pits. His lips were painted red and parted into a ragged, toothy grin. His hair was long, flowing, greasy, and unkempt. His hands were round, like deer bladders full of water, the fingers extending straight out at odd angles. His elbows were even bigger round masses. His forearms dangled from the hideous blackened blobs that were his elbows. They flopped around independently from his upper arms. He moved along more like he was floating, rather than walking. His knees were also blackened blobs of decaying flesh.*

*His lower legs wobbled in all directions as he approached. His manhood stood at full erection and protruded from his groin more than a forearm's length. It was also painted red. The bulbous tip changed and took on the shape of a bear's head, the teeth bared and blood dripping off the fangs. His blackened scrotum hung down like that on a bull moose she had once seen. But it was lopsided, one side hung much lower than the other. A slit appeared in the shorter side and the fletching from Pena's arrow lined the slit. His whole body shined with smelly sweat and bear grease.*

*He dropped to his knees between her outspread legs, and his empty eyes bore into hers. His putrid breath smelled like rotted meat. He tilted his head back and laughed, more like a sarcastic crow calling. Without warning, his manhood drove into her mercilessly. She felt her delicate tissue ripping as he penetrated far beyond what a man should be able to. Through the pain, she helplessly felt a piece of her life soul tear away.* "My baby!" she cried out.

From some distant place, she heard, "Bright Moon...Bright Moon...Bright Moon! Wake up, you are having a bad dream." She recognized Yellow Hair's voice, and her eyes popped open. The room was dark, but she felt Yellow Hair's warmth, drank in his scent. She knew she was awake.

"He was here! He killed my...our baby!" she

blurted out, sniffling. Her cramps continued, unabated.

"Who? Who was here? You have just had a bad dream. I have been here all night."

"He was here! He killed our baby!"

"No. I have been right here, no one but me."

"Thunder Throat was here...he killed our baby!" she cried.

Just then the wall flap to their private sleeping area opened, and the space was lit up by a torch. "What is the problem in here?"

In the torchlight, Yellow Hair looked to Bright Moon. Tears streaked down her cheeks. Her eyes reflected pain and fear. That is when he saw the blood soaking her light fabric sleeping dress below the waist. He panicked. "She needs a healer, go find a healer—fast!"

"My orders are—" He was interrupted by Walks in Moonlight entering the small room with an attendant holding a torch.

"What is the commotion here?"

"Head Matron, he killed my baby!" Bright Moon blurted out, her tears dried up and venom in her voice.

"Who? Who killed your baby? I did not even know you were pregnant." Walks in Moonlight lied.

"Thunder Throat. My old enemy."

"I thought he was dead. You have miscarried your child. It is not uncommon for our young maids to miscarry their first child. Your dream of your enemy is a natural reaction." She turned to her attendant. "Go get Dark Star, my healer. Have her meet us at the Sun Clan women's lodge. Bring back five more female attendants and a litter. This one will need to be carried to the women's lodge." She turned back to Bright Moon. "You will need to spend a few days in the women's lodge. Dark Star, my personal healer, will tend to you. She has healing potions just for these situations. You will be back to normal soon."

"Head Matron, I saw him, I felt him tear my womb, killing the infant that came there to grow. I felt part of my soul ripped from me. He did it, I know it was him." Bright Moon's voice reflected hatred, pain, and fear.

"Dark Star has shaman powers. She will help you sort through all of this. She has medicines that will heal your spirit as well as your body. Go to her and follow her instructions and soon you will be back to normal,"

Bright Moon looked to see Traveler coming into the crowded sleeping room. "Is there anything I can do to help?" He looked to Walks in Moonlight.

"You can make sure Yellow Hair does not do

anything foolish while Bright Moon is in the women's lodge. He needs to stay away from there. Men are forbidden, but I am not sure he completely understands our customs in some areas." She spoke so only Traveler could hear her.

*Something is not right here. There is something hidden behind her words. Something she is not saying. I can see a secret in her eyes. I must be careful in the company of her sorceress. I need to talk to Traveler...alone. If I convey any suspicions to Yellow Hair, he will do something foolish. But Traveler may be able to help me. Or maybe I am just being emotional because I lost my child. How did I get so attached? I did not even know I was pregnant. I have only missed one moon, and that only by a few days...my queasy mornings, my appetite—I was with child, but too foolish to know. Surely my child did not have his own souls yet. He shared one of mine, my life soul...that is why I was so attached. He is gone, and now my cramps are lessening a little.* Bright Moon's mind was racing.

When they got to the women's lodge, Bright Moon was surprised how big it was. *The Sun Clan must be bigger than I thought.* To Bright Moon's relief, the only two people there were an old woman and her young helper. She was glad about that. The attendants got her off the litter, handed the young healer's helper a bag with clean clothes and a few of Bright Moon's personal things, then picked up the litter and left.

The old woman wore a dark, coarsely woven fabric dress with spiral and animal spirit designs sewn in black thread over the shoulders and down the front. Hanging on a peg was a hooded cape of similar design. A large thunderbird design was sewn on the back. Her hair was white and stuck out wildly from her small head in all directions. Her nose was big and hooked like a vulture's beak. A small obsidian crystal was embedded in the side of one nostril. Her eyes were dark and darted from one place to another constantly. Some faded tattoos that looked like bursts of lightning surrounded her eyes, temples, and cheeks. The rest of her face was a mass of wrinkles, her cheeks slender and hollow below sharp cheekbones. Her hard-edged lower jaw and pointed chin accented her toothless mouth. A faded spiral tattoo adorned the tip of her chin. She wore dangling earrings of copper that depicted tiny human skulls. Only her hands stuck out from her long-sleeved dress. The woman's knuckles were swollen and the skin gray and wrinkled. She appeared ancient.

"You are in the presence of Dark Star, Woman Healer of the Sun Clan of the Village of Cahokia. Her medicines and instructions will cure your present infirmary. Who comes before Dark Star for a cure?" The old woman introduced herself in an odd manner.

"I am known as Bright Moon, wife of Yellow Hair. We traveled from the Monongahela lands, past the Spirit River. We belong to no clan. An evil spirit entered my womb and killed my child. I come to you to help me heal so that I may give my husband a son in the future." She hoped that the trembling fear in her souls did not reflect in her voice.

"You need not fear me, child. I am here to mend your body and your souls. First, we must clean you up and get the bleeding stopped. I will have some healing tea prepared soon that will ease your pain. A special gruel will bring back your strength. I have some incense and other things to drive the evil spirits from your life.

"My attendant here will help you clean up and change your clothes. Her name is Sedge, and her tongue is like yours. But do not think you can talk behind my back—I am familiar with all tongues. Sedge, clean this child up and let me know when you are finished." Dark Star turned to the attendant, then walked out to greet Walks in Moonlight outside the lodge.

"I am Bright Moon. I have no clan, but I was born on the Spirit Water River in Long Pine Village. How would you know my tongue?" She spoke in her native tongue to see if Sedge really did understand her words.

"Yes, I know. You killed the murderous Thunder Throat. I came here with my mother's family. My family was one of the farm families along Little Fish Creek. We had no village or clan structure. Just farmers raising enough food to trade for the goods we needed. A moon or so after the raid on Long Pine Village, Thunder Throat came to our farm and accused my parents of hiding you, your sister, and your aunt. They killed my father and raped my mother. Then left us to die. I always hoped that you had lived and then when news came that a maiden had killed a powerful war chief far in the east, I just knew it was you. Thank you." Sedge looked down as she spoke.

"I thought I was glad he would never hurt another soul, but last night, he came into my dream and somehow killed my unborn child." She was shocked that she and Sedge could carry on a conversation in her own tongue.

Sedge said nothing but looked away. *She knows something. I must befriend her,* Bright Moon thought to herself. "Do you miss the hills and valleys of our homelands?" Bright Moon asked, changing the subject when Sedge returned with a pot of heated water and some soft fabric cloths.

"I was very young. I do not remember it well. I miss my father. He carried me around on his back a lot. He taught me how to catch fish and how to make fishhooks from turkey bones. He never beat my mother." It was important to Sedge that her father did not beat her mother but did not know why she told Bright Moon.

"Yes, my father and mother never fought. Our home was happy until that day when it all changed..." She retold the story of Thunder Throat's raid on Long Pine Village while Sedge helped her clean the blood from her groin and legs. Sedge gave her the healing tea and prepared her a net loincloth lined with absorbent moss to soak up the additional blood trickling from Bright Moon's woman hole. A clean dress made Bright Moon feel like a woman again.

"I am sorry you had to go through that. I was younger. I just remember my mother's screams and pleas for them to stop. I do not know how many took her after Thunder Throat was finished, and she has never spoken of it. Once I asked, and she said it was no concern of mine. I have never known a man, and if they are all like those who did that to my mother, I never want to." Again, Sedge diverted her eyes from Bright Moon.

"I have only known Yellow Hair. He is a good man, and I love being his woman. But I have seen many men I want no part of. I cannot answer why some men are good and some are bad to us." Bright Moon sighed. "Is that gruel ready yet? I am hungry." She started to get up. Sedge pushed her back down on her back.

"I will get it. You are to lie here and relax," Sedge said forcefully.

Just then Dark Star came back into the room. "Feeling better already?"

"My pains have lessened some, and my headache is almost gone. Yes, I do feel better. Sedge helped me with the cleanup and getting dressed. Thank you, elder." Bright Moon tried to humble herself as much as she could, considering she was skeptical of the healer.

"The gruel is ready now. Eat some of it and try to sleep—that is what will help you at this point." The old woman sounded confident, but Bright Moon still did not trust her. "Tomorrow we will have some sewing or quill work to keep you occupied."

"I need practice with those skills. I did not spend much time learning how to be a matron as I grew up. I was more interested in hunting and fighting during the years I should have been learning to use a needle." Bright Moon tried to keep the mood light.

"Yes, you wanted to become a mankiller. Now

you are one, and nightmares haunt your sleep. You grow what you plant. We will see if we can teach you how to be a woman, but I make no promises of that happening." Dark Star did not sound supportive.

*They really do hate me here. I do not think I want to spend the rest of my life here,* Bright Moon mused to herself. *At least this gruel tastes good. I wonder if it is poisoned. I cannot detect anything bitter in it. Nevertheless, I think I should eat no more of it.* She handed Sedge the barely touched gruel and told her she could eat no more.

"You hardly touched it. You said you were hungry." Sedge looked at her with a question in her eyes.

"I guess my appetite is not what I thought it was." Bright Moon laid back on the sleeping bench. Sedge carried the bowl back to the fire pit. Bright Moon started to notice that Sedge was getting blurry.

# CHAPTER 24
# WOLF VISITS

Cass awoke in a forest clearing. Her feet were attached somehow to rocks that she could not move. She had a broken war club in her right hand and a broken knife handle in her left. A big black bear approached her huffing and growling as it neared. She could not run. It came up to her, put its face up to hers, and roared. The bear's breath was hot and putrid, like half-digested meat. Without thinking she rammed her left hand into its wide mouth and down his throat, wedging the broken knife handle there. The bear reeled back, gagging and screaming in pain. In his rolling and scrambling, he faded out of her eyesight. She examined her arm and determined it was not injured. She shook all over as she tried to relax, still not able to move her feet.

Movement caught her eye in the forest. Two large

*wolves were circling her. One was black with large, yellow eyes, the other white with deep blue eyes. Soon the white one caught her scent and approached cautiously. As it got closer, it sensed her helplessness and started growling and crouching down to attack. Words came to her. "Wolf, you are my spirit helper. You helped me in my time of need. If you are in need of my flesh to feed your family, I surrender myself to you." She dropped the broken war club and put her hands out to the wolf, palms up. The white wolf answered by springing at her. She had no defense and was driven to the ground.*

*She woke up in a dimly lit room, completely out of breath. Sedge lay on a blanket on the floor a few paces away. Dark Star was nowhere to be seen. Bright Moon lay there catching her breath and feeling her neck where the wolf's fangs had clamped onto her. Her skin was not damaged. Relaxing, she thought, Only a dream.*

*She started to relax when she heard, rather than saw, something slide past the door hanging into the room. She heard footfalls, but they were not human. She tensed, searching for her knife or some other weapon. None was at hand. In the dim light, she saw the black wolf. He was easily the biggest wolf she had ever seen. He gingerly eased over to the sleeping Sedge and sniffed her. Then he turned his attention to Bright Moon. In the dim light, she could see his bright yellow eyes looking deep into her life soul. He approached her slowly, confidently. He sat beside her sleeping bench and looked toward the fire pit. She could see kindness in his eyes.*

*"You chose to fight the bear but submitted yourself to the wolf. Why did you make that choice, child?" The words seemed to come from the wolf.*

*"B-Br-Br-Bright M-Moon could n-never raise a h-hand against a wolf. After all you have done for me, I owe you my life," she stuttered, shaking as she spoke. She wanted to reach out and touch him but was afraid.*

*"Your choice was wise, as has been your habit. But as you have seen, your trials did not end with the destruction of Thunder Throat. You should know that it was squawroot and nightshade that brought Thunder Throat into your dream. It was no action on his part. His souls are so scattered they will never find their way out of the darkness. No, your lost unborn was caused by human interference I am afraid." His voice was the same as it had been in the tunnel ten sun cycles past. She could scarcely believe she was in the presence of Wolf.*

*"But no one knew I was carrying a child. I had not even figured it out myself. I only told Yellow Hair after the baby was lost."*

*"The Head Matron has seen many young maids in their first pregnancy. You bore signs, without doubt visible to her experienced eyes, of which you were*

*unaware. She did not want a child running around who looks more related to a sky god than her own grandchild, so she had your pregnancy terminated. That was the role of the squawroot. The dream, brought on by a small amount of nightshade, deflected your blame to your old enemy. She thought of everything."*

*"I will take a life for a life!"*

*"No, you will not. Destiny will make Walks in Moonlight's grandson the greatest chief in the history of the world. He is to be beloved by people too numerous to count, and he will see to the building of this great city. The squawroot has done its job and ended any competition for Star. Events are taking place that will lead you away from this place. You may choose to go with Yellow Hair to a foreign land that is completely strange to you and your teachings. If you love the light-skinned man, then that is your choice and your destiny. You will be beyond my help there. But I may be of some assistance in getting you there. I can see many children in your future if that is what you wish."*

*"I wish to give Yellow Hair a son and a daughter."*

*"Then you will go with him to the foreign land over the sea. There will be more than a son and a daughter in your future."*

*"Is it Norway?"*

*"No, you will never get that far. You will know hate and mistrust from many of the people you meet. Some*

*will try to harm you. You will need to keep your skills honed. You will kill a woman before you leave Cahokia. She is on her way up the river to kill you right now. Stay vigilant. I must go now."* He got up and walked out of the room without making a sound or looking back.

———

BRIGHT MOON OPENED her eyes to the dim light given off by the coals left in the fire pit. She noted that Sedge was already up and gone. *She must be tending to her personal duties. I must get out of here. I need my weapons.* Just then, Sedge came in with her arms full of firewood.

"Up early this morning." Sedge went about stoking the fire to heat tea and gruel.

"I had dreams, and I must get out of here. My spirit helper came to my dream and warned me about a new enemy I seem to have acquired."

"I do not think Dark Star has any intention of letting you out of here today."

"Can you get Walks in Moonlight to come and talk to me?" Bright Moon tried to sound optimistic.

"I cannot go to the Head Matron and ask her that, no. You will need to get Dark Star to do that for you. I cannot speak for her. I am sorry." Sedge looked at the floor as she answered.

"I need to get moving. At least to get my weapons. I do not know when this new threat will materialize, but I must be ready. You understand that do you not?"

"I wish I could help you. But if I did without permission, my life, and probably my mother's, would be forfeit." A tear streamed down Sedge's cheek as she began to tremble.

"It is alright, Sedge, do not fret. I will figure something out without endangering you. Are these people so cruel? Would they really hurt you for a simple mistake?"

Sedge simply looked down and turned away from Bright Moon. She got her composure back just before Dark Star came into the chamber. "How is the weak one this morning?" The old woman looked to Sedge and knew something was wrong.

"She is feeling better this morning, I think." Sedge did not make eye contact with Dark Star.

"Grandmother, good morning to you. I hope this day finds you feeling well, and the sun shines on your face." After a short pause, Bright Moon added, "I have had a dream and must leave this lodge as soon as you let me go. There are things I must tend to."

"What makes you think you are well enough to

leave my care? What dream? Are you some kind of a dreamer?" Dark Star stared pointedly into Bright Moon's eyes.

"My bleeding has stopped, and I do feel much stronger. I have walked outside and relieved myself and feel I can do normal things. My spirit helper, Wolf, visited me in a dream and warned me of a new enemy coming here to kill me. I must at least be allowed to get my weapons so I can defend myself."

"Wolf! That figures. No wonder you are tied to violence and man-killing. Women should not have man spirit helpers—they poison our souls. I have seen it many times. You must turn your back on this wolf and find a kinder spirit helper. A mouse or bluebird would be better for your soul," Dark Star spat out.

"Wolf has been with me since the night my mother was murdered. I would not, could not, ever turn my back on him. Could you let me talk to Walks in Moonlight about this? I really must get away from this lodge. I need to move so I can be ready when danger arrives."

"You are little more than a child. What do you know of healing?" Dark Star now sounded as if she had been insulted.

"I do not question your methods, Grand-mother. I just know that I must take some action. I will not lie around, waiting to become a victim." Bright Moon could feel her strength returning.

"I will tell the Head Matron. The sooner you are out of my care, the better." Dark Star left the chamber snarling to herself.

A short while later, Walks in Moonlight came into the room with Dark Star. Sedge had just finished helping Bright Moon wash and get dressed. "You may step out until I call for you." Dark Star dismissed Sedge.

"What is all this about an enemy and leaving?" Walks in Moonlight looked at Bright Moon like she was a crazy person as soon as Sedge was gone.

"Head Matron, I was visited in a dream by Wolf, my spirit helper. He told me I would kill a woman who is coming upriver to kill me. After that is done, Yellow Hair and I are to leave Cahokia. We will somehow get to lands controlled by his people, and I will bear many children for him. But my life will be in constant danger by those people. I must go so I can prepare to meet this woman mankiller who seeks me." Bright Moon had the old look of determination and *do not even try to stop me* in her eyes.

Walks in Moonlight began to consider the ramifications. *Must be a Caddoan, they have all kinds of woman warriors and are warlike from the day they are born. Bright Moon could be killed and that would solve what to do with her. She is weak from her miscarriage and loss of blood. Surely she cannot win a fight. With her gone, Yellow Hair will probably do something foolish, and we will be rid of him too. On the other hand, if Bright Moon kills the Caddo woman, she and Yellow Hair will leave us and never come back. Yes, I will let her go. My informants will let me know when this Caddo woman arrives, and a fight to the death can be arranged. I like it. I will tell Far Gazer.*

"Yes, you should go and get yourself ready to meet your enemy." Walks in Moonlight showed no emotion. "Thank you, Dark Star, for taking care of the Sun Clan's guest in her time of need. I will see that you are rewarded. Walk with me to the temple where we will inform Far Gazer of Bright Moon's remarkable recovery."

Arriving at the temple, they found Far Gazer engaged with the building masters discussing progress and plans for future projects. "A word with you, Great Sun," Walks in Moonlight whispered in his ear so that only Far Gazer could hear her.

"What is it? Can it wait? I am rather busy at this time." Not wanting to upset the planners, he whispered out the side of his mouth so only she could hear.

"Clan business regarding our guests. New developments."

"I need to ask you project planners to come back in the afternoon. Something has come up that requires my attention right now. I feel we made good progress this morning and should be able to finish our discussions later." Far Gazer looked down to the four men standing on the floor level of the Sun Temple. "Raven Wing!" When the chief of temple guards came in a few heartbeats, Far Gazer instructed, "Please escort these men to wherever they wish to go and bring them before me right after the sun begins its journey to the western horizon."

"Yes, Great Sun. Follow me, men." Raven Wing turned and walked toward the entrance, asking no further questions.

When they had departed, Far Gazer turned to Walks in Moonlight. "This better be important."

"Watch your tongue with me, son. I can still unseat you. Your power still does not exceed mine." She let that sink in for a moment.

"It seems that Bright Moon thinks she is a dreamer now. She says that a spirit wolf came to her in a dream last night and says she is to kill some woman who is on her way here from the south. The woman is coming to kill Bright Moon, and she wants to leave the Sun Clan lodge so she can prepare for this latest threat. But there is more..." She continued, thrust a hand up when he started to say something.

"This wolf spirit supposedly also told her that right after that business is concluded, Yellow Hair will be taking her off to his world. I suspect the woman coming, if there is one, is from the Caddo lands, where they create many great woman warriors, and is probably at least an equal to Bright Moon. In other words, our dilemma has been settled. We let the two women fight to the death. If Bright Moon wins, her and Yellow Hair leave us with our blessings. If the Caddo wins, Yellow Hair will do something foolish and get himself killed. We are rid of them either way. Dark Star and I have talked and have decided this is a wise course of action for us."

"Our experience tells us that life does not always go along with dreams. Can we be certain that this Caddo will be able to defeat Bright Moon? That seems like the simplest solution to me." Far Gazer spoke without confidence.

The Head Matron thought of Dark Star's recommendation. "Son, I think it would be better if Bright Moon wins. Then her and Yellow Hair will be gone and only one person will be dead. The Caddo people will know it was not one of us who killed their warrior, and they can pursue Bright Moon to the ends of the world if they please."

"There is truth in your words, Mother. I think we should not let this fight take place in the grand plaza. The Cloud Clan still has a courtyard plaza big enough for such an event. Do we have any idea when this Caddo woman warrior will be here?" Far Gazer asked.

"The dream only said she was coming upriver now. I will have my informants keep me abreast of anyone fitting that description's actions."

CHAPTER 25
THE WEST

# CHAPTER 25
# THE WEST

Yellow Hair stayed close to Traveler wherever he went while Bright Moon was in the women's lodge. He was forbidden from entering there and only had a few cryptic messages from Walks in Moonlight's attendants saying that she was feeling better and getting stronger, though it was not known how long she would stay there.

In the company of Traveler's trader friends, Yellow Hair kept hearing stories about the great grasslands that spread to the west. He had difficulty picturing a land so vast with no trees to seek shade and shelter, for making the necessities of life. Yet he kept hearing the stories of the great herds of buffalo, elk, and pronghorns. There are wolves beyond counting and many other animals that thrive on those endless plains. His curiosity rose as he listened to stories of many hunter-peoples who follow the great herds and live their lives tied to the movements of those giant beasts. Yet those stories must be true because Cahokia was filled with buffalo robes, heads, horns, and countless tools made from their bones, and the meat is delicious.

Each time Traveler answered one of his many questions, it just left more unanswered. How did the people find water? How did they make their lodges? How many of them were there? Did spirits tell them where the buffalo went? Did they war with each other over hunting lands?

Finally, Traveler introduced Yellow Hair to Fire Man, a trader who spent each summer with the buffalo hunters and specialized in buffalo trade goods.

Fire Man eagerly explained, "Yellow Hair, you must learn the differences in the grasses that grow across the great expanses where the buffalo thrive. The tall grasses are sweet and full of the things that the animals need in the spring and early summer. The hunting bands each have a shaman who knows the right time and sets fire to large areas. The old growth on the grass burns off, leaving the ground black. The black ground heats faster under the spring sun and new growth quickly follows. The buffalo can smell the smoke from days away and know that fire brings new, sweet grass to eat. In this way, the hunter people get the buffalo to come where and when they want them. Of course, this will only work in the spring." Fire Man enjoyed having someone willing to listen to his long explanations on how things work. He would expound until Yellow Hair cut him off.

"The rest of the year, the herds can be followed by watching the great clouds of dust they make as they trample the grass and loosen the soil with so many stomping over the ground. And of course, after a rare plains rain storm, the mud trail can be followed."

Fire Man chronicled the various hunting methods and explained how the women descend on a kill to butcher it. On those occasions when many buffalo are killed, it might take a hand of days for the women to get all the animals cut up and the meat dried and distributed. Most of the meat from each animal is dried for later consumption, but on some occasions, there is a great feast, and the people eat as much as they can hold. He explained that, in most camps, the hump meat is only offered to men, and it is forbidden for women to eat from the buffalo's hump.

Fire Man and Yellow Hair talked until the sun broke over the eastern hills the following morning.

Fire Man answered all Yellow Hair's questions enthusiastically. Their discussions ranged from the relationship of all the animals, including man, from the tiniest insects to the big beasts and predators to the birds, hawks, falcons, and eagles. Fire Man talked with the same reverence for the vultures and other scavengers as he did for the complex interactions between prairie dogs, burrowing owls, rattlesnakes, and black-footed ferrets.

After the long night of talk, Yellow Hair slipped into Traveler's tent, found a blanket, and fell into a peaceful sleep that lasted until midday. He woke up rested and had a better feeling about Bright Moon's prediction that they would soon be moving west into those vast grasslands. He was ready to experience firsthand the things Fire Man detailed in their talks.

Bright Moon found Yellow Hair where she thought she would—at Traveler's trade booth talking with a handful of traders who were preparing to move farther south for the winter. His armed escort was nowhere to be seen.

"We must talk in private." Bright Moon took his hand and led him to a place away from other people in the plaza.

"What are you doing here? It has only been three days. They said several days after what you went through." Yellow Hair's face showed his wonder and concern. He was most surprised to see her war club hanging from her belt. He grabbed his but did not know why.

"Yes, but they do not know me very well, do they? Let us go for a walk."

They walked toward the chunkey court where no ears could hear them. She relayed her dream in detail and everything Wolf told her. "We must get you away from here before the woman warrior gets here. I do not want you fighting after everything you have gone through lately."

"My trials are far from over, Yellow Hair. I must play it out as Wolf says. He has always guided me correctly. He brought me to you, did he not? If he says I will kill her, then I must. She is a fierce one, I suspect. It matters not. I will do as I must. How will we get to your lands?" She finally changed the subject.

"That part is an open riddle to me. I have seen no ironworks to make the parts needed to build an ocean-going ship. Besides that, I could never muster a crew of these people to sail it. I see no way to make it happen." Yellow Hair looked down and shook his head. "I will think on it. But I still do not want you fighting some strange woman."

"If I can defeat her without killing her, I will. I

212

have no desire to fight a woman, but Wolf says it is my destiny." She was not sure of herself at all.

As they made their way around the chunkey court for the third time, one of the Head Matron's attendants came running up. Out of breath, he blurted out, "The Head Matron sent me to summon both of you to the Sun Clan lodge. We need to hurry."

"Lead the way, we are coming." Bright Moon wondered what new revelation she would find in the Sun Clan lodge.

## CHAPTER 26
# LONG CAT ARRIVES

The sun was nearing the western hills, throwing long shadows across the plaza when Traveler looked up from his friends and saw a short, wide man with an animal skin headdress that tailed down his back. There were three young men following him carrying large trader packs. Even before he could make out his facial features, Traveler knew the man was Long Cat. *What, in the name of all the gods is HE doing here? And at this late date in the sun cycle?* "Greetings, Long Cat! Did the Weroanskua finally put a price on your head?"

"Long Cat knew a ne'er-do-well like Traveler could be found among the biggest liars on the River! You survived the Minquas, I see. Where is that yellow-haired helper of yours? I hope his scalp is not hanging in some Illini Lodge." Long Cat walked up and gave Traveler a bear hug that took his wind away.

Traveler took a moment to catch his breath. "Good to see you, too. You must tell me why you are here in this season. Yellow Hair and his wife are guests of the Head Matron of the Sun Clan, and she sent a runner over here a hand of time ago to fetch them. There was some urgency in the boy's manners. They were out walking and talking about personal stuff, and I saw them leave with the runner at a trot. Something is up, but I am in the dark about what it is."

"The main reason I came down river in this late season was that I have something to show him that I think will interest him a great deal. Especially when I give him the news that goes with it. It is news I do not believe should wait. I also met a chief in Monongahela Village who told me to give you her regards and that she hopes to see you at the Solstice next Moon of the Growing Corn."

"What is it you have for Yellow Hair? I can see that he gets it."

"Oh no. I came this far, I am giving it to him in person, and I am not saying anything more about it. Now, you got some tea and some stew, or must I go begging?" Long Cat smiled as he rubbed his belly.

"I believe both can be found right over here." Traveler guided him to a nearby fire pit.

Long Cat was in the middle of recounting his trip west when a loud ruckus erupted to the northeast across the plaza. They looked and saw a bright glow close to the ground past the Sun Clan lodges. Many people were hurrying to get over there.

## CHAPTER 27
# LIGHTNING

**B**right Moon and Yellow Hair arrived at the Sun Clan lodge and heard a familiar voice talking in a strange tongue. Just as they came into the room, a husky female voice replied to Dark Star. The conversation did not sound friendly. When the woman saw Bright Moon, she became silent and looked her up and down, sizing her up.

The woman was dressed in a dark-tanned hunting shirt with short fringe down the long sleeves. Both sleeves were decorated with white-painted lightning bolts. There were many old bloodstains on the shirt, and it was greasy. It hung down to mid-thigh and was belted around the waist with a buckskin belt from which hung an elk-hafted knife in a quilled sheath and a war club just like Bright Moon's except the stone was black. Her moccasins were nearly black and plain. Her hair was in a single braid down her back nearly to her waist. Though it was mostly black and very shiny, a few streaks of white emanated from a scar in her hairline and flowed the length of her braid. A lightning bolt tattoo adorned each high cheek, and white crystals were embedded in her ear lobes. She stood about the same height and had about the same build as Bright Moon. She posed a frightening image. Bright Moon noted her glaring at her war club.

Dark Star began, "Bright Moon, guest of the Sun Clan of Cahokia, this is Lightning, of the Eagle Clan of Clear Sky Village in the Caddo lands south, down the Grandfather River. The man is Gray Hawk of the Hawk Clan and her companion."

She then switched to the Caddo tongue and introduced Bright Moon and Yellow Hair. Lightning immediately demanded to know what warrior of the True People Bright Moon had killed in his sleeping skins to steal his war club. Through Dark Star, it was explained that Bright Moon got the club from a trader in Monongahela Village up the Spirit River. Lightning maintained that must be a lie. She looked at Yellow Hair and gave a slight, inviting smile, a look not lost by Bright Moon or Gray Hawk.

Lightning then spoke on her own, crossing her arms, tilting her head back slightly and looking into Bright Moon's eyes. She spoke of stories that had reached Clear Sky Village, how some sniveling snake had sneaked into a great war chief's blankets, seduced him, and while he was at the height of his passion, she stuck a bone stiletto into his ribs.

"The story gets better with each telling!" Bright Moon chortled and looked at Yellow Hair with humor in her eyes. She told Dark Star the real story and told her to translate it to Lightning. When Lightning heard Bright Moon's long version, she curled her lips and spat at Bright Moon's foot. Bright Moon quickly moved her foot to avoid the spit and stared back at the woman.

Lightning said she was the greatest woman warrior the world had ever seen, and she would not allow rumors of some eastern camp bitch taking that title from her. She would kill Bright Moon in a fight with witnesses, and the rumors would end.

Bright Moon said she had nothing to prove, and if Lightning wanted to say that she, alone, was the greatest female warrior the world has ever seen, that was fine. She would not contest Lightning's claim and would go about her life.

Lightning laughed hysterically at that and said

that was not an option. If Bright Moon did not wish to fight, Lightning would kill her anyway and take her man. After going back and forth with Bright Moon maintaining they need not fight and Lightning insisting, Walks in Moonlight stepped in and said they would fight it out in the Cloud Clan courtyard just after the sunset and she would hear no more of it. Far Gazer nodded his agreement.

*They think I am going to die. That is why they are agreeing to this ridiculous show. Wolf, I hope you are still with me.* Bright Moon saw what was happening. The Sun Clan needed to be rid of Yellow Hair and his woman to get Cahokia's focus back on them.

# CHAPTER 28

# BLOOD FIGHT

A line of bright torches lined the chunkey court in the Cloud Clan courtyard as the two women prepared to fight. Each would have a war club and a knife. No other weapons would be allowed. The man that accompanied Lightning would stand in her corner, and Yellow Hair reluctantly stood in Bright Moon's. He had unsuccessfully tried to get Walks in Moonlight to stop the fight, but the matron insisted it must go on. The sky gods demanded it.

Bright Moon had put on her plain tan hunting shirt and leggings without fringe. She painted red and white stripes under her eyes. Lightning was now dressed in a sleeveless hunting shirt that was light colored with many blood stains down the front. She had painted white lightning streaks down her muscular arms and added red and black lightning bolts across her cheeks and forehead. She wore the same leggings and moccasins that she had on earlier.

As the crowd gathered just outside the torches, Bright Moon noticed Traveler with a man somewhat shorter and wider. She had no way of communicating with him. She remembered his advice about looking into her opponent's eyes to read their plans. She did not think the strategies she used on Thunder Throat would work on this woman.

At last, Raven Wing called them to the center of the court. Using sign language, he indicated that he would hold his war club up, and when he swung it down, the fight would begin and last until one combatant died.

Bright Moon looked, as best she could, in the yellow light from the torches, for signs of Lightning's intentions in her black eyes. Lightning was doing the same thing as they began a slow circle in the center of the court. Bright Moon slid into that slow-motion world she had when she fought Thunder Throat. The torches stopped flickering, the shouts from the spectators faded away. She looked right into Lightning's soul. She saw a woman who was frightened of failure. There was no thought calculating this move or that one, only a frightened animal that had to kill to live. She almost felt sorry for her adversary.

Suddenly Lightning charged and struck out with her war club. Bright Moon easily saw the move coming and sidestepped with little effort. She countered, and Lightning sidestepped her swing just as easily. They swung their clubs and knives tirelessly for a hand of time. Both had many near misses and close calls. Fresh slices appeared in both hunting shirts. A few drops of blood appeared along a few of those slices, but no real damage was done to either combatant. Both were getting tired to the point of making mistakes, but the other was too exhausted to take advantage. Lightning still glared through hateful eyes, and Bright Moon just looked weary. She was not sure if the moisture in her crotch was sweat or if she had started bleeding again.

Shouts of encouragement rang out from different factions in the crowd, depending on which side they had bet. The spectators could feel the exhaustion of the fighters and knew something would happen soon. The anticipation was reflected in their intensifying shouts of encouragement.

Another three fingers of time slid by as the women attacked and countered with no one landing a solid hit on the other. In the cooling night, both were drenched with sweat. Yellow Hair was increasingly worried about Bright Moon's ability to fend off Lightning's vicious attacks. But she kept deftly slide-stepping or ducking. Her attempts to slap Lightning on the knee or on the back came up empty each time.

After nearly two hands of time, both women could hardly lift their clubs anymore. Swings were becoming more errant, but no less tiring. The crowd was getting restless, and the shouts were getting more heated.

At last, Lightning came straight at Bright Moon holding her club down and back so she could get full momentum into her swing. Bright Moon saw it coming and countered in an attempt to block the swing. At full speed, their forearms glanced off each other, Bright Moon's sliding to the inside. The deflected energy of her swing brought the white rock in the end of her club square into the side of her opponent's head just above her ear. The momentum of Lightning's swing whipped her club around Bright Moon's arm and slapped her just behind the ear. Both women dropped like rocks and remained motionless.

Bright Moon drifted toward the light. Distant noise became louder. Her head felt like a buffalo had kicked her. She heard a familiar voice as her eyes began to flicker. "Bright Moon, come back to me!" Yellow Hair desperately cried out as he held her in his powerful arms. Her body was spent. His hand gently slid over the sore place behind her ear, she could feel the swollen knot there from the way his fingers were sliding over it.

"I think I am all right." Her voice was merely a hoarse whisper. Wobbly, she pulled on Yellow Hair's arm and got to her feet. Lightning lay on her back with a fist-sized hole above her left ear. Blood and brain matter oozed from the hole. Her body was still, and her man was bent over gently wiping her face and crying. He was muttering a chant Bright Moon could not understand. She gently put a hand on his shoulder in an attempt to comfort him, but he pushed her away. However, the hate in his eyes was gone.

Bright Moon stood in Yellow Hair's arms crying. "Why? What was this all about? I do not understand. I tried to make peace with her. She only wanted respect. She had a hard life and just wanted to be someone special. She did not have to die! I never wanted to kill her. I have never killed a woman before." Her voice was a shaky whimper.

"How do you know what she wanted?" He looked down at the dead woman in the arms of her lover.

"I could see it in her eyes before she attacked. This fight should never have happened. I think they wanted me to lose." She began to regain her composure and nodded toward the approaching Sun Clan leaders.

Dark Star told Gray Hawk that the Cloud Clan priests would prepare the woman warrior's body for burial so he could take it back to Clear Sky Village. Gray Hawk held her limp hand and wept.

Far Gazer, Walks in Moonlight, Traveler, and Raven Wing got to Bright Moon and Yellow Hair about the same time. Walks in Moonlight looked hard at Bright Moon. "You frighten me, child. I am glad you are leaving Cahokia." With that she walked away. Far Gazer followed her without saying a word. Only the disappointment in his eyes betrayed his feelings.

"Most impressive." Raven Wing's words were simple as he turned and followed Far Gazer and Walks in Moonlight.

"Bright Moon, I am sorry this kind of thing plagues you." Traveler put a hand on her shoulder and spoke in his most sincere Monongahela tongue.

"It is my fate. Thunder Throat's revenge." Her watery eyes focused on nothing.

Changing the subject, Traveler looked at Yellow Hair. "You remember Long Cat, from the Lenape River? And this is his young helper is Blue Deer, of Lenape Town on the Lenape River."

"Yes, of course. Who could forget that face and that short, powerful body? And pleased to meet you, Blue Deer." Yellow Hair attempted to lighten the mood. He had wrapped a blanket around Bright Moon, but she still trembled under his arm.

"Long Cat says he has a surprise for you and would not divulge it even to me!"

"The message from Wolf," Bright Moon quietly said to Yellow Hair. "We will find our way to your people."

"How can it be?"

"Wolf." Was Bright Moon's only response. As she walked, she knew the moisture in her loincloth was not all sweat. Light cramps returned to her abdomen.

# CHAPTER 29
# LONG CAT'S SURPRISE

B ack at the traders' booths, Long Cat dug through his personal bag and pulled out a fine tanned fisher skin. From it, he pulled out a piece of woven wool. Only Long Cat and Yellow Hair knew it was a hat. Only Yellow Hair recognized the style and weaving as coming from his great-uncle Thorkell's farm.

"Where did you get this!?" The color was drained from Yellow Hair's face.

Bright Moon had never seen such shock and wonder on his face. She had just returned from the creek where she washed and put new absorbent moss in her mesh lining for her new loin cloth.

"I was trading far up north of the headwaters of the Lenape River and met a trader who had come from up on The Great River that Flows to the Morning Sun. He had met a trader who had a bag full of these. He said the northern trader told him of a great canoe that comes each summer to trade a few strips of red cloth, glass beads, and these hats for trees. The men from the great canoe cut the trees and make a great raft from the logs and big limbs. This they tow behind their great canoe to some place that has no trees. I do not understand why they would live where there are no trees. The upper limbs and branches are cut up into firewood for the local people. So far the trading with this great canoe has gone smoothly, but most who come in those great canoes are not friendly and fights break out. I thought you should know this. I think I can get you to someone who can show you the place where that great canoe lands every summer. But since hostilities have broken out between your people and those northern clans, I do not know how long their peace will last. You may want to get there as soon as you can. If you want to go." Long Cat summarized it as best he could. He looked at Bright Moon with that last statement.

"How long would it take to get there?" Yellow Hair's color was back, and he was eager to learn more.

"I think we could get back to Monongahela

Village before the rivers are clogged by ice." Traveler piped up, smiling.

The others looked questioningly at him, but Bright Moon shared his smile. *Corn Stalk is going to have a man!* She kept her thoughts to herself.

"From here I would plan two summers. Travel in the winter in that north country is near impossible. But there are many rivers, and the various tongues are similar to Lenape. With luck, perhaps you could catch the great canoe before it leaves at the end of one summer." Long Cat answered the best he could.

"What are your feelings on this matter?" Yellow Hair looked at Bright Moon.

"My fate is tied to you, husband. Wolf told me I would bear you many children in a strange land across the water. My life will be fraught with danger and hate, but yours will be filled with accomplishment. You will provide well for us in your land, but your people will not trust me. It is our destiny, let us get started. Traveler is right, we need to get upriver before winter hits." She looked into the distance, as if she was watching it unfold.

In two days, they moved their bags and baskets to the canoe landing on Cahokia Creek. Raven Wing and a squad of his warriors escorted them to the landing. "Far Gazer gives his fond farewells on behalf of the Sun Clan. He says that he is grateful

Yellow Hair came to deliver his message. Cahokia will be a more magnificent place for it, and this past Harvest Ceremony will long be remembered by the people of Cahokia. But he also expressed that your welcome here is exhausted. Your woman is too much trouble and will not be allowed to return here. These are Far Gazer's words. I wish you a great and prosperous life."

"Thank you for the warning, Raven Wing. I will always consider you a friend. I doubt if any of us will find a need to return. I know your life under such political constraints is difficult, but I wish you a bright future as well." Traveler hugged his friend and looked around at the city one last time.

Traveler knew great changes would take place over the sun cycles in the growing city. He noted a small ridge-topped mound already covered the grave where the Harvest Celebration funeral pageant had taken place. Apparently the Solstice Pole would be moved somewhere else. Other crews were dismantling the last few old lodges from the grand plaza area. Others were adding baskets for fill on The Great Sun Mound. He could not help wondering how many sun cycles it would take to raise it above the trees, as Far Gazer envisions it. For now, everything was going his way. How long could The Great Sun keep all those people united behind him?

## CHAPTER 30
# UPRIVER

By the time the two canoes loaded with trade goods and personal belongings reached Squirrel Tail Village, the five travelers were happy to have a warm place to sleep. Cold camps coming up the Spirit River and traveling only at night while hunkering down to sleep during the cool autumn weather was challenging. Traveler felt safe enough to negotiate the narrow channel running beside and bypassing Spirit Water Falls in the daytime. It would be extremely difficult at night.

The Hunters' Moon was ushered in with frosty nights and brightly colored days. A brilliant display of fall colors lined the riverbanks and hills above the banks along the Spirit River.

Keeping out of sight and quiet on such beautiful days was difficult for Bright Moon and Yellow Hair. The activities of their choice on those cool days resulted in a long delay in the arrival of her next moon. They would make a happy announcement to Corn Stalk, Water Mint, and Bright Star. Bright Moon was confident this child would be born healthy now that they were away from the scheming rulers in Cahokia. Her nightmares all but disappeared since she and Yellow Hair had committed to one another.

The stretches of bright sunshine were interrupted by a few days and nights of cold rain, strong north winds, and periods of overcast days. The cloudy nights were good for traveling through the Illini lands but more than once they were forced to lay low all night due to brilliant moonlight. As much by good luck as careful planning, they managed to avoid contact with all the hunting parties they saw.

Copper Hawk and two canoes full of young warriors escorted them the final two hands of time as they arrived at Squirrel Tail Village. "Greetings Traveler! And to you, Long Cat and Blue Deer. Yellow Hair, Cass, you are still in the trader's company! Welcome back to Squirrel Tail Village. Grandfather will be surprised, and happy to see you and your company, Traveler. I am sure you have good reasons for traveling upriver so late in the season. Snow will be falling before you can return to Cahokia."

"Good to see you again, warrior. Cass has become Bright Moon and is well married to Yellow Hair."

The warriors helped them pack their belongings up from the canoe landing. When they walked through the palisade's overlapping walls, Traveler noted there were many tracks along with drag marks from many poles. Once inside, he discovered the reason for the heavy traffic. Four new longhouses were under construction and most of the central plaza was covered with temporary housing. *They look like refugees. Many of the men bare wounds. A tragedy has taken place somewhere close by.* He kept his thoughts to himself, as did his companions.

Long Pipe greeted them just outside the Heron Clan longhouse. "Traveler, I am at a loss for words to see you back so soon! I did not expect to see you in these lands for many sun cycles."

"I don't expect to be plying the rivers in many sun cycles, as you put it, old friend. Once again, unusual circumstances have brought me back this way." Traveler wrapped his arms around his old friend and hugged him long and hard.

"Yellow Hair and Cass came along? I thought they would be Head Matron and Great Sun of

Cahokia by now! Long Cat, how did you let yourself get involved with these wanderers?" Long Pipe joked as he led them into the longhouse.

"She goes by Bright Moon these days." Traveler corrected Long Pipe with a wide smile on his face.

"I see. You already noticed some recent changes here in Squirrel Tail. Let's share some tea and stories before evening meal. There is room for all of you to sleep here." Long Pipe gestured to an open area where they could roll out their sleeping skins later. "First things first." He walked over to a woman standing at the head of the elongated central fire pit in the big room of the longhouse.

"Allow me to introduce our visitors from far-off Cahokia. Leader of the group is Traveler, the trader you have heard me speak of often. He claims no clan or village. Long Cat is another trader. The young man with him is Blue Deer, of the Deer Clan in Lenape Town. Long Cat also claims the Deer Clan of Lenape Town over on the Lenape River. They are of the Turtle People in the Lenape world. He travels far and wide, but I believe he has not seen as many places as Traveler has. The young man with the yellow hair and blue eyes says he is a foreigner from lands far across the Great Eastern Ocean. The young maiden is Ca...Bright Moon. Last I heard, she claims no clan or home, but we know she was born in the old Long Pine Village up the

Ohi-yo River, though some still call it the Spirit Water. And to all of you"—he nodded toward the woman— "this is Standing Heron, Head Matron of the Heron Clan, and new Head Matron of Squirrel Tail Village. She is also married to Long Pipe." He gave a contented smile.

"This *is* a lot of news, old friend." Traveler spoke quickly to keep his surprise from being too obvious. "There are many stories to be told indeed." Long Cat's mouth stood open. Yellow Hair looked on in wonder while Bright Moon smiled and nodded politely toward Standing Heron.

"Yes, yes. Let us have a seat, drink some tea, and get to the stories." Long Pipe shared his enthusiasm. He and Standing Heron sat at the end of the fire pit on a flattened log with a deer hide cover for a seat. The guests sat on woven cattail mats on the floor. "Copper Hawk, you are welcome to join us if you have no other pressing duties."

"I need to check on the scouts and get back on the river, Grandfather. We have some nets to put out before dark. Thank you for the offer," Copper Hawk replied, turned, and left.

Standing Heron wore a buff-colored doeskin dress with a standing Great Blue Heron in beadwork on the chest. Her dress was fringed along the sleeves and bottom hem. A plain brown fabric sash tied around her waist showed off her attractive curves. Her gray-streaked hair and the wrinkles around her eyes and mouth betrayed her age more than her body did. Her hair was worn on her head in a simple bun held in place with four slender heron bone pins.

"I welcome you all as guests to the Heron Clan longhouse and to Squirrel Tail Village. Friends of my husband are friends of mine. Our cooks will have a feast prepared by evening meal. In the meantime, we can offer some corn and blueberry cakes with honey if you like. Husband, I think you should begin. I can see that the changes in Squirrel Tail come as quite a surprise to our guests." Standing Heron waved, palm up toward the guests.

"Yes, let me see, where do I begin?" Long Pipe mused. "Raiding and war have become common-place where once we had peace and cooperation. More than a sun cycle past, on the first day of the Green Corn Celebration in Crooked Creek Village where Standing Heron was Head Matron and her husband was war chief, raiders from Red Fox Creek Village attacked. Those villages lie several days north of here. The Crooked Creek warriors were caught by surprise and fought desperately to repel the raid. Crooked Creek lost some good men, including the war chief. A few Crooked Creek granaries were emptied, and some women and children were taken. The Crooked Creek Village Council decided to rebuild what they could and conducted a retaliatory raid, which was successful. That gave them the ability to make it through last winter and plant their fields this past season. It almost seemed like things were getting back to normal, except Standing Heron had not yet found a suitable husband." He looked to his new wife for approval of his telling.

"However, the Red Fox Creek Villagers were able to recruit some more warriors and raided once again on the first day of the very next Green Corn Celebration. The results were even more devastating. This time Standing Heron's daughter and her granddaughter were taken. The surviving elders decided to come to me asking for help. They did this as Standing Heron is my previous wife's younger sister. Of course, we took them in and, as you can see, are building longhouses for the four surviving clans.

"As soon as lodging is secured, we will go on a war walk to rescue the slaves taken in the raid. It is probably too late to help the six warriors taken alive. Since Standing Heron had lost her husband, and I had lost my wife, we saw our marriage as a good way to tie the two villages together as one. It seems a good arrangement." He smiled at her. "Her ten-and-seven warriors added to Squirrel Tail's ten-tens will make a force the Red Fox Creek defenders will not be able to repel. Now, what brings you back our way just before the snow flies?"

Traveler told of the adventures they had encountered from the time they had left Squirrel Tail Village until they returned, including Long Cat's encounter with a trader from far in the north. "The possibility of Yellow Hair getting back to his own people was too inviting to pass up."

After listening carefully to every detail, Standing Heron wanted to know more about Yellow Hair and Bright Moon. Traveler spent another hand of time telling a condensed version of their stories from start to finish. She listened carefully for Traveler to be done. "I have heard the story of Cass but did not realize Cass and Bright Moon were the same person." Standing Heron's curiosity was evident.

"Bright Moon was my child name, but that childhood ended on that horrible night. It seems a lifetime ago, but that night is still fresh in my memory. I wish it were otherwise. Yellow Hair liked Bright Moon better than Cass, so I went back to that name for him. I will admit that it does bring back happy memories of my childhood days." Bright Moon lost her focus while she talked.

"And Bright Moon has no fear of going off to Yellow Hair's foreign land?" Standing Heron asked.

"He has adapted to this world all right. I believe I can adapt to his as well. My life is where my husband is." She held his hand up and smiled.

"You are a remarkable young woman, Bright Moon. I wish you well." Standing Heron gave her a motherly smile.

"Thank you, Head Matron." Bright Moon's eyes deflected to her lap in embarrassment.

"As you saw earlier, our chunkey court is temporarily being used for lodging, so a rematch is out of the question I am afraid." Long Pipe changed the subject.

"Were it not important for us to get to Monongahela Village before winter sets in, we would stay and help you build longhouses." Traveler looked at Long Pipe. "We should be on our way as soon as possible. We do not wish to overstay our welcome. You have much to do and we do not wish to burden you." Traveler turned his attention to Standing Heron.

"Good friends are no burden, Traveler. But I understand you wanting to get to your destination on these cold nights." A knowing smile crept across Long Pipe's face. Bright Moon smiled inwardly—she understood the reason for Long Pipe's comment.

# CHAPTER 31
# FAMILY

T wo mornings later the five travelers were back on the Spirit River moving upstream. Long Pipe had ensured them it would be safe to travel by day between Squirrel Tail and Monongahela Villages. They encountered fewer farm steads and clusters of lodges as they made their way upriver. The hills lining the river grew higher as they traveled. The brilliant autumn colors were beginning to fade as they advanced into the Moon of Falling Leaves. Most nights were frosty, and their campfires did little to warm their sleeping robes those nights they did not bother putting up shelters.

Yellow Hair and Bright Moon kept them in good supply of meat and gathered nuts while they were out hunting. Deer, turkey, and grouse were plentiful, and the river was blackened with migrating ducks and geese. The hard part was not killing too many animals for their ability to eat and store the meat.

Bright Moon's routine began by retching each morning when she left the men to tend to her natural needs. She was repulsed by morning stew and always made the excuse that she wanted to scout around for signs of human activity while the men ate. It only took a few days for them to figure out what was going on, and they left her alone. Yellow Hair waited impatiently for her to break the news to him that she was carrying his son once more. *This time there will be no powerful clan to secretly end her pregnancy, and we can celebrate when the baby comes.*

As the days grew shorter and the nights grew longer, colder air settled on the river. They awoke one morning to a sky as gray as the rocks exposed on some of the hillsides. Through the morning, a cold north wind whipped white caps on the river surface. They had to hug the bank to keep the canoes from capsizing. Making matters worse, they were in the stretch of the river that flows south so they could do little to avoid the wind and waves. After struggling a couple hands of time, they decided to pull up and camp in a sheltered grove until the storm passed. They built a lean-to on the west side and banked the north wall with cedar boughs. By the time their camp was secure, and they had a small fire going, wet snow began to fall. When dark came, the slushy wet snow turned dryer and piled up a finger deep by sunrise the next morning. The sky was still solid gray and hung low, light snow continued to fall.

"It is too early in the season for this weather to last very long. I say we wait here for the storm to pass." Long Cat leaned over the fire pit. "I am too old for this. I should have stayed with Long Pipe. Good spirits made a home in his soul."

"Long Cat, I think you would enjoy building longhouses in this weather as much as you do paddling your canoe into a hard, north wind."

"Well Traveler, at least there I might have found someone to warm my blankets on these cold nights. That would take my mind off the misery." Long Cat scowled as he laid out his sleeping robes.

By the time the snow finally stopped falling and the sky began to lighten in the west, another finger of snow lay on the land. "The tracking should be good." Bright Moon was ready for a hunt.

"Exactly why we should travel no further from this shelter than we need to." Traveler quickly ended her plans for fresh venison.. "No one needs to know that strangers are lurking around in these woods."

"Good point." Long Cat added.

"Look, the sun is breaking through the western sky. I think tomorrow we can travel again." Yellow Hair tried to change the subject.

Bright Moon was checking the lines and stones on her bola. "Looks like ducks for evening meal again. Permission to use the canoe, Chief Traveler."

"Just do not leave any tracks on the water."

"Funny."

A hand of time later, Bright Moon and Yellow Hair were back with four mallards and two canvas-back ducks. The party would eat well again.

When the north wind swung to the southwest, the temperature climbed dramatically. The pines, spruces, and cedars drooped from the weight of the wet snow, and the deciduous trees sagged. Many of the colorful leaves fell from the weight of the snow on them. By the time they had their camp packed up and the canoes loaded and ready for launching, the temperature had climbed well above freezing. The floor of the woodland sounded like rain was falling. But the sky was blue, and a warm, soft, southern breeze would help push them up the river. Late in the day, the snow was but a memory, and they were making good progress.

The river turned northeast before they camped

that night. "If this weather holds, we will make Monongahela Village in less than ten days. Your stew is getting better, Bright Moon. Or it has been so long since I have had good stew to compare it to?"

"Thank you for the compliment, kind elder. Let it be known that anyone who wishes to do the cooking for this party is welcome. Otherwise, tell your complaints to the woodland spirits."

"Can I see the wool hat again, Long Cat?" Yellow Hair turned his attention to Long Cat.

"You ask to see it most every night. Can you not remember what it looks like?"

"I just want to reassure myself that it is my uncle's weave." Yellow Hair wanted to be certain he was doing the right thing, dragging Bright Moon across Turtle Island and all the way to Greenland. He still did know how long it would take them.

Long Cat dug into his bag and pulled out the protective skin. Before he handed it to Yellow Hair. "Your hands must be clean."

"They are." Yellow Hair carefully took the hat and turned his back on the others as he painstakingly looked at each stitch. Bright Moon noted the slight shudder in his broad shoulders and knew he wept for his lost family. She turned and made small talk with Traveler and Long Cat so that he could have his private time. She managed to keep her own tears out of their sight, as she felt his pain.

The false summer lasted well into the Moon of Falling Leaves as the forest trees were slowly denuded of the past summer's foliage. When the rising smoke columns of Monongahela Village came into view, only the oak trees with their reddish-brown and golden-brown hues and the evergreens gave the hillsides a contrast from the drab gray of the lifeless deciduous trees. The vultures had been replaced by kettles of migrating hawks in the skies. The annual migration of water-fowl was near an end, but skeins of ducks and geese still winged their way up and down the big river.

They had seen a few small harems of cow elk accompanied by their bull along the river. A pair of fighting white-tailed deer bucks had become hopelessly entangled with each other and lay dead on the riverbank. Wolves or coyotes and other scavengers had reduced them to bare spines with skulls and meshed antlers left to tell the story. Beavers frantically hauled fresh cut willow branches to riverbank burrows, and otters played as if there was no tomorrow to worry about.

Only two canoes of five young warriors joined them after they rounded the last bend, and the canoe landing came into view. It was midday, and the sky was mostly sunny with a few white clouds drifting eastward. The temperature was cool with a westerly breeze that sharpened the air a little more. Sliding their canoes onto the gravely canoe landing, they were met by Red Oak.

The first thing Red Oak noted was the fresh deer carcass lying in Traveler's canoe that Cass and Yellow Hair were paddling. "Greetings, friends! This is an unexpected surprise indeed. Did you bring your own food supply?"

Red Oak noted the newly painted white hands on Traveler's bark canoe and the white lance with three newly painted white feathers on Long Cat's dugout. "Looks like there is still trouble in the Illini lands."

"Never hurts to be careful. The deer is a gift for the Head Matron."

"Drake, you and your men, carry the guests' bags and baskets up to Corn Stalk's longhouse. And be careful of everything in them. Get a pole to carry the deer to the back of the longhouse so the women can butcher it." Red Oak's authority over these young men was evident.

Bright Moon broke and ran up the slope to the flat ground when she saw Corn Stalk approaching. Corn Stalk wore her blue doeskin dress with a darker blue, long-fringed cape over the shoulders and arms. Her hair was in a single braid wound on the top of her head and held in place with carved turkey bone hair pins. She also wore a bright smile when she saw who came to visit her village.

Bright Moon approached Corn Stalk, who spread her arms and took Bright Moon in a full embrace. "So good to see you healthy, grand-daughter. I see you brought your usual company, plus another trader or two. Have you become a trader yourself?"

"So much has happened these past few moons, I think it is better we discuss it over tea—inside where it is warm."

"Greetings, traders!" Corn Stalk's smile could not be contained as the others walked up. "Let us go in where it is warm, and I want to hear your stories."

"Head Matron, we have brought a fresh-killed deer for your lodge. It is yours as a gift from our party."

"An unneeded gift but appreciated. Thank you, Yellow Hair," Corn Stalk noted Yellow Hair and Bright Moon stayed close to one another. *I assume they are married now. I have many questions.*

Once they were all seated along the fire pit in Corn Stalk's longhouse, she had the attendants serve everyone tea, corn cakes flavored with blue-berries, and cattail root cakes flavored with walnuts and pecans. A jar of honey was passed around for additional flavoring. "Who is the spokesman for your party?" Corn Stalk looked to Traveler. *There is something new in his eyes, hmm.*

"How much do you want to hear, Head Matron?" Traveler's demeanor was somehow changed. *Is he going to announce that he has a wife waiting in Cahokia?*

"I wish to start." The beaming smile on Bright Moon's face could not be contained.

"Yes, Granddaughter." Corn Stalk cocked her head in surprise.

"First, I took my old name back. I am known as Bright Moon again. Also, I am the wife of Yellow Hair...and I carry his child in my womb!" She finally unleashed her excitement with the announcement.

"In the names of the gods, my heart sings for you! You are a good provider?" Corn Stalk turned to Yellow Hair.

Before he could reply, Bright Moon proclaimed emphatically, "The best!" Her face beamed with pride.

"And you have come here to have your child? Or are you plying the rivers with traders?" Corn Stalk could not contain her fears for Bright Moon.

"I will let Traveler tell our story from when we left your canoe landing last spring." Bright Moon settled down, knowing that Corn Stalk would not agree that it was all good news being shared this day.

Corn Stalk looked to Traveler. He relayed everything that happened going down river to Cahokia, then the events that took place right after their arrival. He emphasized the importance of The Great Sun's Second's burial, explaining that it was the spark the current Great Sun needed to expand Cahokia to an even larger, more powerful citie. People from all over the world would migrate there to be a part of the wonders taking place and those yet to come. Far Gazer predicted spectacular Sky World events for the time when his son, whose arrival coincided with Yellow Hair's, would be re-quickened as The Morning Star himself. Traveler told her that people will be awestruck by the power and closeness to the gods that the rulers of Cahokia will appear to have.

He then got back to the role Bright Moon and Yellow Hair played in the assassination and were honored guests in the Sun Clan lodge. He told her how things turned sour when the Head Matron concluded that Bright Moon was pregnant. She secretly had the pregnancy terminated by mixing squawroot into Bright Moon's food. Then a Caddo woman came to prove that she was a better warrior than the mankiller known as Cass. Bright

Moon not surprisingly was able to defeat the woman.

"That same day, Long Cat and Blue Deer showed up in Cahokia with the news that brought us here. It seems that members of Yellow Hair's clan have been trading the past few years far in the northeast with relatives of the Lenape, who Yellow Hair was rescued by. So Yellow Hair and Bright Moon, with the help of Long Cat, determined that they would seek those Norse traders and try to get to his homelands. Traveler condensed the story, trying not to leave out important details.

"What of her? What of her homeland, her family?" Corn Stalk asked anxiously. "Bright Moon, you have faced so much danger for one so young. You should stay here to raise your children. You and Yellow Hair would be a welcome addition to this village, or New Long Pine." Tears filled her eyes. She knew Bright Moon was lost in Yellow Hair's arms and would do as he bid.

"Grandmother, my place is at my husband's side. He was robbed of his family and country at a young age. If he has a chance to get back, I will accompany him." Bright Moon left some of Corn Stalk's questions unanswered.

"Where do you intend to spend the winter? Where will you have your child? In a canoe on a river somewhere I suppose. Will you at least see your sister and aunt before you leave us forever? They are both with child also. Did you know that? I expect your ability as a seer would have shown you that."

"I did not know, Grandmother, but my heart sings for all of them. Yes, we intend to see them." Bright Moon gave Corn Stalk her old, determined look.

"Head Matron, could I have a word with you in private?" Traveler interrupted.

Corn Stalk looked at Traveler with tear-filled eyes but saw something there she could not determine. A sincere beckoning. One she felt she must answer. She slowly got up and moved toward the door hanging to her private chamber. He followed her instantly.

When they were out of the range of the other's ears, she turned to him, looking vulnerable, weak. A tear trickled down her cheek. "I do not want to lose her again. Where are you taking her?"

"Head Matron, a long time ago, you asked me why some matron had not lured me in and made me a chief." He let her memory search for that conversation.

It brought her back to her sweat lodge. "You brought me in here to seduce me? Your needs must be great." Sarcasm filled her voice and her eyes.

"I came to tell you that such a matron has

captured my heart. But there is more I want to discuss with you right now. I have never been a great believer in gods directing our lives. I always believed humans made their choices and either blamed the gods or gave them credit for the consequences. But watching things unfold with Bright Moon and Yellow Hair has given me a new perspective. It is like they are pieces in some game and some outside force is moving them, guiding their actions without their knowing. At the same time, those forces are protecting them. For what purpose, I have no idea. But it seems no action by other humans fazes them. They are good people with generous compassion for others, yet both can kill with no more thought than us killing a mosquito. I cannot explain it. But I have come to the conclusion to let the gods take them where they will. They are not made to follow the rules of our society, only the will of who or whatever is guiding them. Our place is to let them go. Believe me, my heart aches as yours does, but I know they must do what they must—I am powerless to stop them." Traveler spoke into her face as he held her shoulders, making her look into his face.

She saw the sincerity there. "You are going with them to Yellow Hair's world? Your fate seems to be tied with theirs." Her voice was barely a whisper.

"That takes me back to my first statement. I told you that a matron has captured my heart. That matron has never asked me to stay, nor has she told me there is a permanent place in her lodge for me. I am not sure of her heart's desire." He kept his eyes focused on hers, searching her souls.

"And if this matron took you into her lodge, how long before the longing to be on the river again takes you away? What assurance does she have that you would not leave as quickly as you came?" Her questions hit him like the point of an arrow.

"She has only my promise. I hope she has always seen the truth in my words in the past. I intend to give my canoe and most of my trade goods to Bright Moon and Yellow Hair to help them with their long journey to...who can say where?"

"Is it not in your heart to see them to the end of their journey? Do you not wish to see this Greenland?" Corn Stalk's voice softened.

"My shoulders and back tell me I can no longer keep pace with their youthful strength. It is time for me to be thankful for the things I have seen and to spend my time serving the person who makes my heart feel fulfilled. To use my knowledge to make someone's life better—yes, to assume clan responsibilities." His reply brought a warmth to her heart and tears to her eyes.

"Traveler's heart is full of surprises." Corn Stalk took a deep breath. She looked up at her curved ceiling for several heartbeats. Moisture filled her eyes. Finally, she continued, still looking up. *Not since my late husband died have I dared think another man would share my life. Now I feel like I am gifted by the gods with someone to carry me into old age. Thank you, Creator.* "Yes, Traveler, there is a place in my lodge for you. Our wedding will take place before Bright Moon leaves us. Your place in the village will be decided by the Council of Elders by Midwinter Celebration. Shall we go back and announce that I will take you as my husband?"

"You are Head Matron. I am happy standing anywhere in your presence." He smiled as his own eyes filled with moisture.

"After your old bones have rested for two nights, we will accompany Bright Moon and Yellow Hair upriver to New Long Pine Village. We will have a great feast there to celebrate the changes in all our lives." She beamed, took his hand, and led them back toward the big room in her longhouse. "Are you sure you want to give up your canoe?" she asked, looking at him for hesitation in his bearing.

He quickly and frankly answered her. "He did

as much work on it as I did. It is half his, anyway, and I no longer am in need of a trader's canoe." She squeezed his hand tighter.

———

THE SHADOWS WERE long six days later when their party of six paddled their three canoes into the New Long Pine Village landing. From the landing they had to walk a finger of time up the path to the bluff where the new palisaded village stood. When they reached the overlapping wall entrance they were greeted by a handful of young boys and girls eager to take them into the village. Corn Stalk was a familiar face to them, and each wanted to hold her hand as they entered.

Bright Moon and Bright Star hugged each other so hard it took their breath away. Bright Star's bigger belly made the hug a little awkward. Tears cascaded down both their faces, and no words were exchanged. When they finally pulled apart, Water Mint repeated the whole scene. Her third child would come before midwinter, Bright Star's in the Awakening Moon. Bright Moon's would not come until the Moon of Ripening Corn.

In a hand of time, the introductions were completed, and the men separated from the women, each group talking about things pertinent to them. In short order, slabs of venison and several turkeys were roasting around the central fire pit. Even before everyone had consumed all the food they could eat, drums began pounding out a rhythm, and people started dancing.

Water Mint cried her congratulations to Corn Stalk for taking a new husband. She knew better than to question the sanity of marrying a trader.

Bright Moon waited until a quiet moment the next day when the four women were alone to announce the plans that brought her and Yellow Hair up the Spirit River. Water Mint and Bright Star looked at her in shock, their mouths open and slack jawed. "How? Why...?" Bright Star tried to formulate a coherent question but was unable to.

"Yellow Hair, who will retake his childhood name, Tor, lost his whole life out in the Great Eastern Ocean. Now he has been given a chance to reclaim part of it, at least. I could not deny him that chance. I will walk with him into the jaws of the Horned Serpent if that is what it takes to make him happy. He is a good man, and he makes me feel whole. Our hearts beat as one." Bright Moon patted her belly as she finished.

"It just sounds so dangerous to take a child into those frozen lands!" Water Mint exclaimed. The others looked at her with wonder in their eyes.

"I think my sister knows what danger is, aunt.

If Wolf tells her that is where she must go, then she will do it, and whatever dangers await her had better be cautious. I have a terrible feeling that once she crosses that water, there will be no coming back. But she must follow her destiny wherever it leads. As we all must." Bright Star spoke out, ending with her wet eyes and her hand on her own growing belly.

"I have come to the conclusion that it is useless to try to talk Bright Moon out of doing anything, dangerous or not." Corn Stalk was beginning to understand Bright Moon.

"You will walk in my heart and in my mind always." Water Mint finally realized that Bright Moon would do what she felt was right, no matter what anyone said.

"And all of you, as well as those no longer with us, and all those who come in the future, will walk in my heart, mind, and dreams as long as I breathe." Bright Moon responded with the only words that came to her mind. She patted her belly to emphasize her meaning.

The men's conversations dealt with the realities of traveling into the unknown and the harshness of the weather where Yellow Hair was taking Bright Moon. Long Cat assured them that his trading connections could get him there and that those people were well adapted to the climate, as

Yellow Hair's people must be. His only concern was if the great canoe still came to the bay to trade in the summer. If it no longer did, then Yellow Hair and Bright Moon would make their way back.

"It seems like a great gamble," Red Hand interjected.

"And was it a great gamble for you to provide information to Bright Star so that your Great War Chief could be defeated?" Yellow Hair looked at Red Hand.

"We all take great chances and make big changes for the ones who truly matter in our lives." Traveler looked into the dancing flames in the central fire pit. All nodded, thinking about their own lives.

"Did you note the moon dog last night?" Tallow changed the subject. "In a couple days, snow will be falling. I hate to be the one to break this party up, but you all should be getting the Head Matron back to Monongahela Village before winter settles in."

"You are right, of course." Traveler marveled at the wisdom of all the young men around that firepit. The men started for the new Water Plant Clan longhouse. The village was arranged in a big circle at the top of the bluff overlooking the river. A palisade surrounded a space large enough for ten longhouses and some smaller buildings. At the time only three longhouses had been built, along with four smaller round dwellings. Smoke rose from the smoke holes in the roofs of each building. The village was small, but vibrant, and Traveler felt it would grow in the coming sun cycles.

The next morning the visitors said their good-byes before setting a rapid pace down the river they all now called the Ohi-yo rather than the old Spirit Water. The old peoples who had given it that name were mostly displaced, and the newer name was more popular among the current inhabitants of the valley.

All but the very eldest and some caregivers of New Long Pine Village undertook the journey to Monongahela Village to attend the wedding of Head Matron Corn Stalk and Traveler.

The large party made their way down river trying to beat the storm they knew was coming. On the third day they woke up to a leaden sky in the northwest. The cold air and wall of clouds descended on them faster than they could paddle. By midday the wind changed from a southeasterly breeze to a cutting northwest wind. The temperature dropped from being comfortable in a long-sleeved hunting shirt to bone-chilling cold in a finger of time. Cold mist transformed into a cold downpour by midafternoon.

They decided to pull into a sheltered cove and

set up camp as best they could and wait out the storm. Sharing all of their tent covers, they were able to set up shelters that would keep them all dry. Outside the tents they set up deer hide lean-tos that protected their small cooking fires and made places to dry firewood.

Overnight the rain slowed to a freezing mist that quickly coated everything. The hard north wind did not let up, and the sound of breaking branches and limbs echoed through the forest. They spent the whole next day stuck in their ice camp while the freezing mist continued to build up the coat of ice on every exposed surface. By nightfall, the mist had stopped, and the air stilled. The entire world seemed lost in a thick, frozen fog. The breaking limbs eerily sounded throughout the night. Twice during the night, smaller branches fell on their shelters sounding like great rockslides. By good luck, the skins and supports of their shelters withstood the falling branches, and no emergency repairs were needed.

The next morning, they woke to a clear blue sky and warming temperatures. The light southerly winds quickly turned the frozen forest floor into a quagmire. The melting ice dripped on them constantly while they packed their wet belongings into the canoes. They were happy to be on the river paddling again. The movement and strain of paddling soon drove the cold from their muscles. Late in the afternoon, they approached the campsite at the mouth of the Kiskiminetas River where Yellow Hair and Traveler met the party from Black Bear Village some eight moons past. With their clothes almost dry, they found enough birch and cedar to build roaring fires to help dry out their tents and sleeping skins. Another half day of paddling would bring them to Monongahela Village and the dry longhouses.

# A LOOK AT BOOK FOUR
## JOURNEY TO ICELAND

**In a tale of endurance and discovery, two warriors must face the perils of a world divided by sea, culture, and fate.**

After navigating treacherous lands and forging bonds across Turtle Island, Tor and Bright Moon set their sights on an even more dangerous journey—one that will take them across the vast ocean to the distant Norse colonies of Greenland and Iceland.

But with weather, prejudice, and the ghosts of old enemies threatening their progress at every turn, they must find a way to prevent the permanent expulsion of their people from the lands they once sought to explore. Yet, as they race toward a distant bay and refuge, the weight of their journey—and the realization of what may never come—begins to bear down on them.

With each step forward, Tor and Bright Moon must decide whether their shared hope is enough to forge a new future—or if their journey will end in a world forever fractured by division.

*Embark on a breathtaking journey of resilience and heartbreak as two determined souls fight to carve out a future in a world at odds with itself.*

**AVAILABLE JANUARY 2025**

# ABOUT THE AUTHOR

Ron Briggs is a veteran, having served four years in the USAF. His education includes a Bachelor of Science in Range and Wildlife Ecology at Oklahoma State University and a Master of Science in Range and Wildlife Management at Texas A&I University.

He is retired from the USDA-Natural Resources Conservation Service, and his career encompassed twenty-five years as District Conservationist in Linn County, Kansas. Prior to college, he worked seven years in the building trades.

Having developed a deep interest in history, especially in the pre-colonial period of North America, Ron's interests prompted him to begin researching a pre-history story about the Tallgrass Prairie Region of the Great Plains. That research evolved into his current multi-volume work, the Yellow Hair series, which includes scenes from northern Europe to the mountains of western North America.

Ron and his wife, Debbie, currently live in Mound City, Kansas, and have two grown children and seven grandchildren. His interests include spending time with family, writing, hunting, fishing, traveling, and woodworking.

# BIBLIOGRAPHY

Appelt, Martin. "Man, Culture and Environment in Ancient Greenland." Publication No. 4, Danish Polar Center.

Bierhorst, John. *Mythology of the Lanape: Guide and Texts*. University of Arizona Press, 1995.

Bronsted, Johannes. *The Vikings*. Penguin Books, London, 1960, Revised 1965.

Clarke, Helen and Bjorn Ambrosiani. *Towns in the Viking Age*. St. Martin's Press, New York, 1991.

Cohat, Yves, tr. Ruth Daniel. *The Vikings: Lords of the Seas*. Gallimard, 1987.

Damas, David. *Arctic, Vol. 5, Handbook of North American Indians*. Smithsonian Press, Washington, D.C., 1984.

Charles River Editors. *Native American Tribes: The History and Culture of the Inuit (Eskimos)*.

Feasel, Charles T. *White Bear*. Ballantine Books, New York, 1990.

Fitzhugh, William and Elizabeth Ward. *Vikings, The North Atlantic Saga*. Smithsonian Press, Washington, D.C., 2000.

Gordon, E. V., rev A.R. Taylor. *An Introduction to Old Norse*. Oxford Press, London.

Gronnow, Bjarni. *Late Dorset in High Arctic Greenland: Final Report on the Gateway to Greenland Project*. Canadian Archeological Association, 1999.

Grumet, Robert S. *The Lenapes (Indians of North America)*. Chelsea House Publishing, 1989.

Harrington, Mark R. *Religion and Ceremonies of the Lenape*. Forgotten Books, 2012.

Harrington, Mark R. *The Indians of New Jersey, Dickon Among the Lanapes*. Rutgers University Press, New Jersey, 1966.

Heckewelder, John Gotlieb Ernestus, notes by William C. Reichel. *History, Manners, and Customs of The Indian Nations*

# BIBLIOGRAPHY

*Who Inhabited Pennsylvania and the Neighbouring States.* Historical Society of Pennsylvania, 1881.

Ingstad, Anne Stine et al. The Discovery of a Norse Settlement in America. Excavations at L'Anse aux Meadows, Newfoundland, 1961-1968. Tromso, 1977.

Jones, Gwynne. *A History of the Vikings.* Oxford University Press, 1968, 1973, 1984.

Kunz, Keneva, tr., edited by Gisli Sigurdsson. *The Vinland Sagas.* Penguin Books, London, 2008.

McCullough, K. M. "The Ruin Islanders: Thule Culture Pioneers in the High Eastern Arctic." Archeological Survey of Canada, 141, Canadian Museum of Civilization, 1989.

McGee, Robert. *Ancient People of the Arctic.* University of British Columbia Press, Vancouver, 1996.

McGee, Robert. *The Last Imaginary Place.* Oxford University Press, New York, 2005.

Mcleod, William Christi "The Family Hunting Territory and Lenape Political Organization." American Anthropology 24.

Maschner, Herbert, Owen Masson, Owen, and Robert McGee.*The Northern World AD 900-1400.* The University of Utah Press, Salt Lake City, 2009.

Maxwell, Moreau S. *Prehistory of the Eastern Arctic.* Academic Press, New York, 1985.

Means, Bernard K. *Circular Villages of the Monongahela Tradition.* The University of Alabama Press, Tuscaloosa, 2007.

Rasmusen, Knud. *Eskimo Folk Tales.* Gyldendal, Copenhagen, 1921.

Roesdahl, Else. *The Vikings.* Penguin Books, New York, 1987.

Schledermann, Peter. *Crossroads to Greenland, 3000 Years of Prehistory in the Eastern High Arctic.* The Arctic Institute of North America of the University of Calgary, 1990.

Seaver, Kirsten A. *The Frozen Echo, Greenland and the Exploration of North America, ca. A.D. 1000-1500.* Stanford University Press, Stanford, CA, 1996.

# BIBLIOGRAPHY

Simpson, Jacqueline. *Everyday Life in the Viking Age*. Dorset Press, New York, 1967.

Sutherland, Patricia, ed. *Contributions to the Study of Dorset Paleo Eskimos*. Canada Museum of History, 2005.

Trigger, Bruce G. *Northeast, Vol 15, Handbook of North American Indians*. Smithsonian Institution Press, Washington, D.C., 1984.

Weslager, C. A. *The Delaware Indians: A History*. Rutgers University Press, New Jersey, 1972.